IBBY SCOTT & REBECCA WESTCOTT

ALL the

PIECES

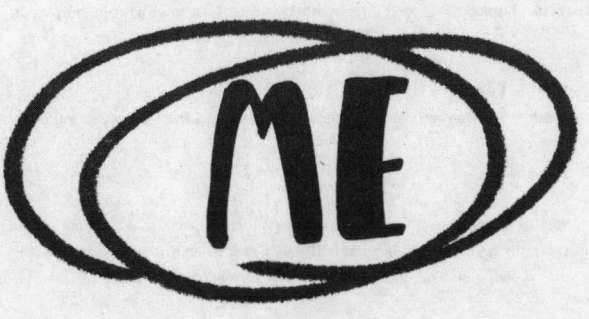

ME

SCHOLASTIC

Published in the UK by Scholastic, 2022
Euston House, 24 Eversholt Street, London, NW1 1DB
Scholastic Ireland, 89E Lagan Road, Dublin Industrial Estate,
Glasnevin, Dublin, D11 HP5F

Text © Libby Scott and Rebecca Westcott, 2022
Cover lettering by Aaron Cushley, 2022

ISBN 978 0702 31741 5

A CIP catalogue record for this book is available from the British Library.

Printed by CPI Group (UK) Ltd, Croydon, CR0 4YY
Paper made from wood grown in sustainable forests and other controlled sources.

1 3 5 7 9 10 8 6 4 2

www.scholastic.co.uk

PROLOGUE

Shhh. Stay very still for a moment and listen to the sounds around you. What can you hear? Maybe people are laughing nearby, or your teacher is telling the class to open their books and read the first few pages. Perhaps someone else in the room is watching television or playing music or trying to get your attention and it's hard to concentrate.

But try.

What else can you hear when you really focus?

The hum of traffic outside the window or a dog barking further down the street. Birds chirruping in a distant tree. Footsteps outside the door. A clock ticking down the minutes to lunchtime.

The inhale and exhale of your own breathing.

The pounding of blood in your veins.

Do you know how many sounds the human ear is capable of hearing at any one time? It's a lot. And when you stand in the middle of a noisy classroom you are hearing every single sound that is being made. But you aren't *listening* to them all. Hearing is the sense we use to process sound but listening – that demands something more entirely.

Listening is about paying attention.

It's about making a thoughtful effort.

Listening is so much more than hearing, and everyone does it in their own way, whether they can hear sounds or are hard of hearing or deaf. Because listening is not just about the things that can be heard. It's about watching and feeling and understanding. It's about paying attention to the things that *aren't* being said.

And listening is what you're going to have to do if you ever want to know what it is that Tally Olivia Adams has to say.

Because the words that come out of her mouth are only half the story.

CHAPTER 1

They are everywhere she looks. Some of them are prowling in gangs, stalking their prey. Others are screeching and shouting and generally attempting to be the loudest they can possibly be while randomly kicking a football at each other. On the far side of the field a whole crowd of them are caught up in an activity that involves chasing after their allocated victim and rugby-tackling them to the ground. It doesn't appear to have any actual rules – none that Tally can figure out, anyway. She suspects they're making it up as they go along, which is absolutely the worst kind of game, in her opinion.

Not everyone is in a group, though. Scattered here and there are the loners. The ones without their people, which is why they're standing on the edges

1

of the field. It's always important to have a couple of escape routes when you're the prey, and they know it. The whole scene reminds Tally of the zoo, and she wonders for a moment why people don't buy tickets to visit their local high schools to observe the students in their natural habitat.

"And here we have the Alpha male, banging on his chest and bellowing loudly as he runs after a ball." She puts on her best David Attenborough voice. "As you can see, if another male approaches him he is instantly threatened and, despite the fact that this is generally understood to be a non-contact activity, he will stop at nothing to take out his opponent – including punching him in the face, if that's what it takes—"

"Did you hear what I said, Tally?" Lucy's voice cuts in. "Or are you off on another planet, as usual?"

And then there are the girls that *she* is sitting with. The popular, confident, pretty girls. Tally isn't one of them, she knows that, but her best friend Layla is, and so Tally gets to hang out on the edges, not quite part of the group but not on her own either.

"Planet Tally," sniggers Jasmine, giving Tally a sideways look. "Where all the aliens live."

Tally blinks and tries to focus on what Lucy had

been talking about. Something about her new haircut, perhaps?

"It looks great!" she says, making sure that she sounds enthusiastic. "Honestly! I really love your new fringe!"

Lucy rolls her eyes and, next to her, Ayesha makes a snorting noise. "I wasn't talking about my *hair*," Lucy tells Tally. "Keep up, will you? I was telling everyone about how my YouTube beauty videos are really getting noticed."

Tally has a YouTube channel too, but her account is private and she hasn't got any followers. That's OK, though. She writes her songs and performs them on her keyboard to make *herself* feel good, not anyone else. She has considered that maybe it would be nice if people heard her every now and again, but the possibility of being made fun of is just too great to risk sharing her music with anyone else. The only person she *ever* shows it to is her dad and even then it makes her feel nervous.

"I got a ton of followers last weekend after I posted my nude make-up tutorial…" Lucy looks around the group of girls, clearly waiting for their response.

"It *was* incredible," agrees Ayesha.

"You're going to be *so* famous," gushes Jasmine.

"Well done, Lucy," adds Layla.

"Why were you *nude*?" asks Tally. "That's a bit embarrassing, isn't it?"

It's a joke. *Of course* it's a joke. Tally might not have the slightest interest in make-up or any of that stuff, but she hasn't survived the last almost-thirteen years without developing a *few* skills, one of which is using humour to join in with a conversation. People like it when you make them laugh.

Lucy stares at her for a moment and then flicks her hair over one shoulder.

"It's a type of *make-up*," she explains, over-enunciating, as if she's talking to a baby. "It's where you use neutral colours that match your skin tone."

"No, I know—" starts Tally but Ayesha shuffles forward on the grass and shoves her face right into Tally's.

"I'm wearing nude make-up today," she says, her hot cheese-and-onion breath making Tally wince. "Look. Can you tell?"

Tally tries not to breathe as she looks obligingly at Ayesha's skin.

"Sorry," she confesses after a long minute. "I can't see anything."

Ayesha laughs. "Exactly! You're not supposed to be

able to tell I'm wearing it. It took me *ages* to get ready this morning but I followed Lucy's tutorial and it really works!"

"Turn to look at me," orders Lucy. Ayesha obeys and Lucy peers closely at her face, her eyes critical. "You messed up this bit around the brows," she informs her best friend. "I'll put up a video on 'Everyday Eyes' and that should help you." She runs her finger along Ayesha's cheekbone and bobs her head up and down, reminding Tally of a chimpanzee grooming its child. "But this is pretty good, for a beginner. I can barely tell you're wearing any make-up."

"So what's the point, then?" asks Tally. "If nobody can see it."

It's a fair question, but Lucy raises a perfectly shaped eyebrow, as if Tally is being ridiculous. "To hide what you really look like, obviously."

Tally frowns. "But why would you want to do that? There's nothing wrong with either of your faces."

Ayesha gives her a big smile. "It's OK for people like *you*," she says, her voice dripping with apparent kindness. "*You* don't think that way and *you* don't mind how you look. But some of us get really insecure about stuff like spots and blemishes."

"And that's why make-up is important." Lucy stretches out her legs and picks a bit of grass off one knee. "It makes sure that nobody can see your imperfections."

The faint sound of a ringing bell drifts across the field and Layla glances at her watch.

"Period five is about to start," she groans, reaching for her bag. "Why does lunch always go so quickly?"

Tally couldn't disagree more. The sixty minutes of lunch always passes so, so slowly for her, unlike the hectic, manic pace of lessons where she barely has time to figure out what subject she's supposed to be learning before it's time to move on to the next.

The four girls stand up and start walking back towards the school building. Tally pauses for a second before slowly pushing herself off the grass and following them, their words tumbling around her head and turning themselves into question after question.

Why does Ayesha think that she doesn't care what she looks like?

Who are *people like her*? Surely Ayesha can't be suggesting that all autistic people aren't bothered about their appearance? Tally isn't interested in make-up but that doesn't mean how she looks isn't important to her, and being autistic hasn't got anything to do with it. It's just her.

And what did Lucy mean about make-up hiding a person's imperfections? Tally definitely isn't perfect, she knows that, but she also knows that some lipstick, mascara and eyeliner isn't going to go anyway near hiding the parts of her she isn't so proud of.

Being friends with Layla is one of the most important things to Tally in the entire world, but she seems to spend most of her time desperately trying to keep up with all the rest of them and Tally's been wondering for a while if it's really worth the effort. Their biology teacher told them a few weeks ago about shoals of fish who stay in a big group for social reasons. He said that some fish, like herrings, get very anxious if they are removed from the group. Tally is definitely a little herring, swimming on the edges of a big shoal, trying not to get left behind. It's a long way from the group of friends she found on last year's school camping trip but that's just the way it is. She bonded with Gory and Jade over their mutual love of animals and they have become two of her closest friends, but they don't go to her school and since she drifted back to swimming with Lucy and Ayesha, she's barely seen Aleksandra, even though she's in year eight too. Lucy and Ayesha don't ever actually say anything bad about Aleksandra, but Tally has seen the way they flick glances between them whenever she stops to say hello to Tally and Layla. It makes Tally feel worried and uncomfortable, and it's just been easier to let Aleksandra drift away. If it wasn't for Layla, pulling her along behind her, Tally would be completely out in the shadows and all alone.

She glances again at the loner kids. Some of them are listening to music through their headphones and one of them is walking into school with his head still buried inside a book. Maybe being alone wouldn't be so terrible? Or perhaps she and Layla could form their own group, just them? Two people is all you need.

"Come on, Tally!" calls Lucy from up ahead. "I'm not getting a demerit card just because you walk at the pace of a snail."

Ayesha and Jasmine laugh, and even Layla beckons at her to speed up. Tally hesitates, trying to figure out if they're mocking her, then breaks into a jog. She's lucky to be part of a group, even if she is on the edges.

She just didn't expect to feel quite so lonely.

Hi, Readers!
In this first issue of TALLY magazine we meet the legend herself, soon-to-be famous pop star, Tally Olivia Adams!

Tell us about yourself, Tally.

Well, what do you want to know? Tally is short for Natalia, which is my real name. I'm twelve (almost thirteen) and in year eight at school. I love dogs, horses, Taylor Swift and I'm just like any other nearly-thirteen-year-old. With a bit of a difference.

Ah, yes, are you talking about your autism diagnosis? Tell us about that.

Finding out I was autistic when I was ten was a mixed bag for me. I learnt more about who I really was, and why I'd felt so different, and I gradually started to own my autism rather than be ashamed of it. But it did take some getting used to. I'm autistic with a PDA profile – which stands for Pathological Demand Avoidance – and that means I really struggle with everyday demands and expectations, and with not being in control of situations. And, yeah, yeah, I know what you are thinking: we all feel like that. But this is different. It's not your usual not-wanting-to-do-something. It's pathological, which is a horrible way of saying that it's extreme. Very extreme. Very, very. And pretty exhausting at times too.

What are the trickiest things you are handling right now, Tally?

That's an easy one to answer: friendships. And being at school. Oh, and having a family. Just those. Everything else is OK.

Tell us about more about friendships.

Well, it's strange how you can be right in the middle of a group of friends but still feel completely alone. I do have Layla, who is never horrible to me. She understands me, which is all I want in life really. Unfortunately, with me that doesn't happen very often. Layla is so popular that everyone wants a piece of her so I have to share her with the others, who don't make me feel so comfortable. Kids like Lucy and Jasmine make me feel edgy, like when they say nice things about my clothes even though I know they aren't cool. Lucy gets this sort of menacing beam across her face which makes me think what she says isn't as genuine as the words she's saying. I hate not being sure if someone means what they say or not. It makes me feel really uneasy. But, hey, I guess I'll take fake compliments if it means I manage to stay in a friendship group, even if it feels like I only have a ticket for the back row.

How about school?

I'm kind of used to it now, and I don't mind the lessons soooo much ... at least I sort of know what's expected of me (unlike at break), and I like some teachers and I think they like me. So they should – I work hard to try and do the right things. Not getting into trouble is the main focus of my days at school, because getting into trouble is the most humiliating, excruciating thing. All those eyes burning into you as you get told off – aaargh, it's making me stressed just thinking about it.

What would you change about school?

If only I was allowed to choose what I want to learn and how to learn it, school would be amazing. When my mum does her evening classes, there's a whole pamphlet that she can choose from showing different types of lessons. That's how school should be for young people too. I actually love learning, just not the way they make you learn at school.

I taught myself to speak Spanish when we were on holiday because I wanted to understand people, to skateboard because I wanted to get around faster, to play the piano and guitar and ukulele and drums because I wanted to write and perform my own songs, and to mimic EXACTLY the sound of the ticket machine at our local train station – just because it was fun.

But apart from a few teachers, like Mrs Jarman, Kingswood Academy isn't interested in what you already know and already can do. They're not even interested in what you would like to be able to do. They just decide everything for you. Where to sit, when to talk, even when you can go to the toilet or take off your blazer. Honestly, it's true, folks. Then they say they are teaching us to be able to think for ourselves! What a joke. Next question, please.

OK, update us on your family.
Mum is working more and is busy and stressed, and I feel I don't get enough nice time with her at the moment. Nell is also being really annoying and needy because she has exams coming up and so Mum and Dad are bending over backwards to be nice to her. For some reason, every

time they say something lovely and positive about her it instantly makes me feel like they are making a negative point about me. Even though I know this isn't really the case, my brain alerts me that it might be.

And then there is Dad. He sometimes gets it wrong with me, a bit more than Mum does, but at least he listens and tries. Mum says he's just worried about stuff, which makes me worry. I try to be less difficult. But it's my brain I have to convince, and that's not so easy.

CHAPTER 2

Rupert is waiting for Tally when she and Nell dash in through the front door, both desperate to get out of the rain. He bounds up to her on his strong three legs, his tail wagging with excitement.

"Good boy," she murmurs, bending down to stroke his soft head, as pleased to see him as he is to see her. He never lets being a bit different bother him and Tally often wishes that her life could be as simple as his.

It's been a long day. Between navigating tricky conversations with the girls, she has also had to deal with being forced to read aloud from the class book in English and a horrible PE lesson with Miss Perkins, who still seems to think that Tally is always looking for an excuse to get out of games because she's lazy. All of that, combined with struggling to understand how to subtract algebraic fractions in maths but not wanting to draw attention to herself by asking for help, which means that she now has no clue about how to do the homework, has filled her stress bucket almost to the brim. All she wants is to snuggle up with Rupert, eat some biscuits and then maybe write a new song or perhaps message with Gory and Jade in their Cat Appreciation Group Chat. If she does that then there's a good chance she can open the tap at the bottom of her bucket and let some of the stress leak away.

"Oh, you *do* have a voice, then," says Nell, shrugging off her coat and hanging it on one of the hooks. "I was beginning to think you'd lost the power of speech."

Drip. Nell's sarcasm drops into the bucket.

"No." Tally straightens up and glares at her. "I just didn't want to talk to *you*."

Nell opens her mouth in a retort but is interrupted by Mum coming out of her art studio, her face marked with streaks of paint.

"Hi, girls!" she says, giving them a big smile. "How was today?"

"Exhausting," groans Nell. "My coursework deadline for textiles is in two weeks and it's still not quite right and I'm super stressed and I'm never going to pass."

Mum puts her arm around Nell's shoulders and pulls her in for a hug. "We could look at it together, if you think that might help? But first let's get you a drink and a snack – we need to keep your energy levels up before the exams start!"

Tally sighs. Nell is constantly exhausted and constantly super stressed and constantly whining about how she's going to fail everything, even though, as far as Tally can work out, Nell has never failed a single thing in her sixteen years of charmed life. But Mum eats up every word and fusses around her oldest daughter like she's getting ready for a mission into space, not just sitting some stupid GCSEs.

"I'm going to stay on after school for the next couple of days and go to revision club," Nell tells Mum as they walk down the hallway. "So Tally is going to have to come home on her own. Is that OK?"

They both glance back at Tally, who is still standing next to Rupert.

"I guess that will be fine?" Mum says, her voice doubtful.

Tally frowns. She hates it when people do this – say one thing when they quite clearly mean the opposite. It's a waste of words and a waste of time. If Mum thinks that her walking home alone is genuinely fine then she shouldn't be saying it like a question. And how *can* Mum say that it will be OK when she can't possibly know that? Anything could happen to her if she has to come home without Nell. She could get kidnapped or hit by a car or attacked by a gang.

Drip. Another drop falls into her bucket.

"She'll be all right," says Nell, giving Tally what is presumably supposed to be a reassuring smile. "It'll be good for her to have a bit of independence – she's in year eight now and it's embarrassing for her to be collected by me at the gates, like a baby."

Nell and Mum disappear into the kitchen, but Tally doesn't move a single muscle. She couldn't move right now even if she *wanted* to because every tiny part of her is frozen in place. Her feet, her legs, her arms, her neck – none of them can move. And the inside of her body is even worse than the outside as the freeze creeps into her veins, finding the fastest route to her heart where it settles, cold and heavy like a cloak made of ice. Even her stress bucket has stopped rippling and is now a solid mass, benumbed and glacial.

She doesn't want more independence. She just wants to be *safe*.

She isn't a baby. She just worries about people being mean on the walk home when there are no parents or teachers or big sisters to stop them saying whatever they want.

And she hadn't even *thought* about feeling embarrassed that Nell collects her from the gates at the end of every day. Not until Nell put the idea into her head.

The flood of heat into her cheeks thaws the ice. Her limbs become free, her heart flames and the glacier melts, surging upwards with such force that it almost takes her breath away as it threatens to overspill the confines of the bucket.

Tally tries to take deep breaths as unwanted images burn themselves on to the insides of her eyes. People pointing at her and thinking that she's weird.

Drip.

Other kids laughing at her for walking home with Nell.

Drip.

Nell hating every single second of time she's forced to be with her, like Tally is some kind of troublesome burden.

Drip.

Drip.

Drip.

Her fists clench and she blinks furiously because more drops of anything aren't what she needs right now. And she won't cry, but it's not that she isn't upset – she's angry with herself for getting it wrong, yet again. She keeps thinking she's got it all figured out and knows what's expected of her, but then something like this happens and she's reminded once more that she hasn't got a clue. It's so, so easy to mess up and not even know until it's too late. And *too late* usually means other people's mockery and snide comments and even more distance between her and them.

And there is already such a fine line between being part of the group and being a loner – Tally knows, because that is exactly where she spends most of her time, at school *and* at home. Maybe she should just get it over with and strike out on her own, before she's pushed out? She could be like an intrepid explorer or a wild adventurer, forging her own path and doing it all her own way.

"I'm fine to walk home on my own," she declares loudly, marching down the hall and into the kitchen. "I didn't want Nell waiting for me every day anyway. I hate having to listen to her banging on about her boring day."

Nell flops on to a chair and rolls her eyes. "Yeah, whatever."

"That's great," Mum tells Tally. "And Nell's right. You're probably ready for a bit more independence now and it'll help get you prepared for next September when Nell goes off to college."

Drip.

Tally swallows hard and says nothing. All anyone can talk about in this house is precious Nell and her precious exams and her precious place at college. Tally doesn't even know what to think about the fact that Nell won't be at Kingswood Academy next year. She might be the world's most irritating sibling but at least she's there.

The back door opens and Dad rushes inside.

"It's raining cats and dogs out there," he says, shaking the water from his jacket. "How is everyone today?"

Nell launches into yet another monologue about the pressure of school and Tally gazes out of the window, wishing that it really *was* raining cats and dogs. When she was younger, she used to believe it when Dad said that phrase and she'd rush excitedly to the window only to be disappointed by the lack of new pets in the garden. Rupert is great but she'd have five dogs if Mum would let her, and ten cats. They could live in Nell's room, and her boring sister could live in Dad's shed.

"I've managed to book us a table at that new restaurant in town," Dad tells Mum, once Nell finally stops to take a breath. "They had a last-minute cancellation for tonight, just for the two of us."

Mum gives him a smile, but her lips are stretched tight, like they actually want to turn into a frown. "That sounds nice. Although it might have been a good idea to check with me before you went ahead and made the booking." She turns to Nell. "Are you happy to babysit Tally this evening?"

Drip. Only babies need babysitting. Mum should know better than to use that word.

Nell nods. "I'm going to be revising anyway," she says. "So as long as she doesn't interrupt me or make any noise then it should be fine." She turns to Tally. "You can't have the living room," she warns. "I want to spread out all my textiles work on the carpet. You can be in your room or the kitchen."

"But what if I want to watch television?" Tally's voice is quiet. "I can only do that in the living room."

Mum brings a glass of orange juice to the table and puts it down in front of Tally. "You can watch something

21

on your iPad in your bedroom," she tells her. "Nell's revision really does have to come first."

"No." Tally stares at the table, not looking at anyone else. "That's not fair and I don't want you to leave me with Nell."

The interesting thing about stress buckets is that you can fill them a lot more than you might think. Maybe experiment with a glass sometime, just to see. Fill the glass with water, almost to the brim, and then keep adding more, a tiny bit at a time. Drop after drop after drop and even when it seems certain to spill, the glass just keeps on taking more to the point where it's impossible to believe that it has any room left. The water forms a kind of skin and seems to rise above the lip of the glass, completely full but contained, hanging on for dear life.

But it only takes one drop to push it a step too far and when it falls, it isn't only that drop that will overflow. The tiny one-drop-too-far opens a floodgate that allows all the other drops to cascade down and, before you know it, the water is gushing over the side of the glass and causing chaos, like a mini Niagara Falls. And, the thing is, the one-drop-too-far doesn't even have to be anything major. It can be something really, really small and insignificant – something that on any other day really wouldn't register as a big deal.

Because it isn't really about what triggered the final drip. It's the fact that there is literally no room left in the bucket.

"*Here we go*," mutters Nell darkly. "Yet another drama-filled evening courtesy of the drama queen herself. *Brilliant*."

"Nell," warns Mum, but it's too late. The one-drop-too-far is suspended in the air for a long, strained moment and then it plummets down, down, down, splashing into the bucket and sending all the stresses of the day, which have been so precariously balanced, plunging down the sides.

The room is still for a moment as everyone holds their breath, waiting to see what will happen next. Tally waits too. If anyone was ever interested enough to ask, she would have told them that this is almost the worst part of a situation like this. The seconds before she knows how her head is going to react to the myriad emotions that are swirling around her brain. The seconds before she knows what response she's going to have, in order to keep herself safe.

Maybe she'll freeze up, like she did in the hallway

earlier. That often happens when she's confused and not sure what she's done wrong.

Or perhaps her body will protect her by putting her into fight mode. Her muscles will tense, and her mouth will open and she'll be a whirlwind of chaos and noise before collapsing in an exhausted heap on the floor. That can happen when she's scared and anxious.

Or maybe she won't freeze *or* fight. Maybe her brain will opt for a third option; an option that it's only started choosing recently but which is much easier than the other two.

Tally's legs start to twitch and before anyone can react she's up and out of the chair and bolting through the kitchen door. She races down the hallway, ignoring Dad's shouts and fumbles with the handle on the front door, but it won't budge. Sneaky Nell must have bolted it at the top when they came in. Well, the bolt might slow her down, but it isn't enough to stop her.

"Tally!"

She ignores Mum's voice and stretches up on her tiptoes, reaching for the bolt, her fingers just grazing the metal.

"Tally! It's OK."

The bolt slides back and she yanks at the handle,

just as Dad pushes past her and leans his entire weight against the door, blocking her path.

"Get out of my way!" she screams at him.

"You are not leaving this house!" he tells her, voice firm.

"I hate you!" Tally pounds on the door with her fists, not caring when several of her thumps land on Dad. "I hate all of you. Just leave me alone!"

"Well, that's lovely," he says, flinching when another blow lands on his arm. "But you are not running away again and that's final."

He takes hold of her hands and tries to hold her still, which makes the terror inside Tally rear up. She wrenches herself away and presses her body against the wall, her breath coming in short pants as she struggles to get enough air into her lungs.

"Just give her a minute," Mum tells Dad. "You're making the whole thing worse."

Dad makes a noise that sounds somewhere between a laugh and a sob.

"*I'm* making it worse?" He looks across at Tally, who is glaring at him with narrowed eyes. "I'm not sure it could *be* much worse."

"She's still in the house and she's safe," Mum

murmurs, although Tally's senses are on heightened alert and she can hear every word. "It could *definitely* be worse. Let's give her some time to recover. She's overloaded right now."

Tally lets her back slide down the wall until she's sitting on the carpet, her knees pulled up tightly to her chest. He should have let her go. All she wanted was to find a sanctuary, a safe place where she could let the stresses of the day leak quietly away. If Dad hadn't tried to stop her then none of this would have happened. Flight is so much kinder to her body and her head than freeze or fight – but nobody seems to understand her need to run when things get too much. They're only ever concerned about it making *them* feel bad, not the fact that it helps *her* feel better.

"The table is booked for seven o'clock," says Dad, finally moving away from the front door. "We've got plenty of time."

"You're joking, aren't you?" Tally looks up to see Mum staring at Dad with an odd expression on her face. "We can't go out now. Not after this."

Dad sighs loudly and flings his hands out in front of him, as if he can't believe what Mum is saying. "So is this the way it's going to be? Us being held to ransom by the tantrums of a twelve-year-old? Never able to do anything that she doesn't like?"

"They aren't tantrums," Mum hisses back at him. "You know that."

Dad shrugs and in that moment Tally thinks that she really, properly hates him – not just words-that-come-out-in-the-middle-of-a-meltdown hating but feeling-it-in-her-bones hating.

"She needs you to understand," Mum says quietly. "*I* need you to understand."

Dad's shoulders slump and he reaches a hand towards Mum.

"I'm sorry," he tells her. "I just wanted to have an evening with you where, maybe, just for once, we could pretend to be regular parents of regular kids and relax a little bit."

Mum reaches out her hand as well, but they're too far apart and the space between them is too big. "I don't know, regular kids sound a bit boring to me," she says, her voice carefully light. "Who wants to be regular when you can have all this excitement for free? Would you really want to change anything?"

"Of course not," Dad says quickly. "I wouldn't want to change a thing."

He smiles at Mum and then down at Tally and she can see straight away that the words coming out of his mouth are fake. Dad is lying and Tally knows it.

He *would* want to change something and that something is her.

CHAPTER 3

Tally can hear the argument as she walks down the stairs. She slows down and steps as silently as she possibly can towards the kitchen. The door is firmly closed and they aren't shouting, but even so, the tight, strained words push themselves through the gap between the door and the floor, where they scurry about, like sinister beetles.

"I just think you should take *my* side for once," hisses Dad.

Tally presses her ear against the wood and listens.

"It's not about *taking sides*," snaps Mum. "And it would be a lot easier to back you up if you'd just take on board some of the strategies that we've been given for dealing with her."

Her.

That means they're talking about Tally. She's noticed

29

this happening more and more often, at home and at school. People using Tally's name less and "*her*" or "*she*" more often. It makes her feel like some kind of impersonal problem and not a real person.

"*Strategies!*" Dad's voice gets louder. "That's exactly what I'm talking about. I'm a *father*, not a strategist. I just want to parent my child now and again without having to worry about whether I'm using the latest professional guidance or expert advice. You know, like we do with Nell."

"Tally isn't Nell, though, is she?" Mum sounds frustrated. "They're two entirely different children and we need to approach our parenting differently."

Dad huffs, his unspoken words scuttering under the door and scrabbling around next to Tally's feet. She knows exactly what they're saying.

Tally isn't Nell.

That's the whole problem.

"We can't keep going on like this." Mum is quieter now and Tally leans in to listen even harder. "It's not fair on the girls and it's not fair on us. I'm *tired*, Kevin. I spend all my time fighting the school and the local authority for extra funding and enhanced provision, and I can't fight you too. I can't keep doing this. I need a *break*."

The sound of footsteps in the hall makes Tally look round.

"Are they arguing again?" asks Nell, leaning against the wall beside her.

"Shh," whispers Tally, holding her finger up to her lips. "I'm trying to listen."

Nell rolls her eyes. "You *do* know that eavesdroppers never hear anything good about themselves, don't you?"

Tally ignores her. She never hears anything good about herself even when she isn't snooping.

There is the sound of a chair scraping across the floor and then Dad's voice, closer to the door this time.

"What are you trying to say, Jennifer? What do you need a break from? From me? Us?"

Mum's response is impossible to hear but seconds later the back door slams and then there is only silence. Tally pushes away from the door and gazes at Nell, her eyes wide.

"Are they going to be OK?" she whispers. "Why would they fight like that?"

Nell stares back, her cheeks flushed red and her jaw clenched tight.

"They'll be fine," she murmurs. "Don't worry about it."

"*It?*" Tally's stomach roils and rolls like a ship on the

ocean and she steps forward, searching her big sister's face for clues. "What is *it*?"

Nell sighs deeply, her breath lifting her fringe from her forehead.

"Nothing. Everything is going to be OK. Maybe just try to give them some peace for a while, yeah? Be a bit less … oh, I don't know…" Nell runs her hand through her hair and wrinkles her nose at Tally. "A bit less *full-on*, if you know what I mean?"

And then she turns and heads up to her room and Tally is left on her own. She pulls her sparkly blue headphones from around her neck and puts them over her head, but even her favourite Taylor Swift song can't stop Nell's words from ringing in her ears.

Be less full-on.

She has no idea how she's supposed to be less of herself, but it's obvious that Nell thinks Tally is part of the problem so she's going to have to figure it out.

The walk to school with Nell is silent, which is a good thing because Tally's head is tangled up with so many emotions that she can't even *begin* to unpick them. All she can do is concentrate on finding enough energy to get through today so that she can go home, cuddle with

Rupert and figure out what she needs to do to stop her parents from arguing, which it would seem is going to have to involve her *not being her*.

Layla is waiting for her at the school gates as usual, chatting animatedly to Lucy, Ayesha and Jasmine. Something is different, though, and the nearer Tally gets, the slower her feet become as she watches Layla's hands waving in the air, the expression on her face definitely not the same as any other boring Wednesday morning.

"There you are!" squeals Layla, spotting Tally loitering behind Nell. "Hurry up, Tally! I've got big news!"

Tally's feet stop moving entirely. Nell shoots her an annoyed look and then plods off in the direction of the art rooms, leaving Tally standing alone on the pavement. She's already had to deal with Mum and Dad arguing this morning, and even though Layla seems excited, there is a buzzing sound in Tally's ears which is telling her that she's probably about to hear something that she isn't going to like.

"You won't believe what's happened!" Layla races down the pavement and clings on to Tally's arm, dragging her towards the gates. "My parents told me last night and I was going to message you but Lucy thought it'd be more fun if I told you face to face!"

"Isn't it amazing?" calls Lucy. "I'm well jealous."

"Shh – I haven't told her yet!" Layla pulls Tally up to where everyone is standing and then releases her arm to reach into her bag, pulling out a piece of paper.

"This is the clue!" she announces, jiggling from one foot to the other. "Can you guess? Mum and Dad made me work it out but it took me ages!"

Tally stares at her, trying to interpret Layla's words. She hates puzzles, Layla should know that.

"Look at the *picture*," says Ayesha. "Guess where Layla's going!"

Tally tears her focus away from Layla's thrilled face and makes herself look at the photograph.

"It's Mickey Mouse," she says, feeling stupid.

"And where does Mickey Mouse *live*?" asks Lucy, her voice patronising.

Tally shrugs. "Disneyland. Or Disney World? I don't know."

Layla giggles. "Well, he actually lives in both, but this picture is of Disney World in Florida!"

"Have you figured it out yet?" laughs Ayesha. "Where it is that Layla is going?"

Tally frowns. This is starting to feel uncomfortable. If Layla is going to Disney World then she could have just told her. There was no need for all this drama.

"So, you're going on holiday to Florida?" Tally nods at Layla. "Have a good time."

Lucy makes a wrong-buzzer noise, as if Tally is on some kind of quiz show.

"Uh-uh. You get one point for the correct answer of Florida but zero points for saying she's going on holiday."

"It's so incredible!" whoops Layla, unable to contain herself any longer. "We're moving to America, Tally! I'm going to live in Florida!"

Tally stares at her best friend, unable to speak.

"Her dad got a new job!" says Jasmine.

"She's going to be in *seventh grade*!" Ayesha grabs hold of Layla's hand and does a little dance. "It's so exciting!"

Layla pulls away from Ayesha and skips across to where Tally is standing. "Well, say something!" she laughs, sounding a little nervous. "What do you think?"

What *does* she think?

She thinks that Florida is filled with alligators and bears and rattle snakes and that it all sounds quite worrying.

She thinks that Florida has hurricanes which are very different to an English storm, because English storms don't usually involve houses being knocked down or blown away.

She thinks that America is a very long way away and she is probably never going to see Layla again.

She thinks that if Layla is gone then she really will be left with nobody and she can't believe that after everything they've been through together she's about to lose the one person who truly gets her.

She thinks that Layla seems really happy and that's good because Tally loves her best friend.

She thinks that she has got to *not* think about how much this hurts and just be pleased for Layla. And then Layla will hug her and tell her that they won't lose contact and maybe she'll invite Tally to Florida in the summer holidays and Tally won't utter a word about the weather or the deadly animals or the utter betrayal.

Tally opens her mouth, ready to speak; ready to say the right thing.

"I think that it—" she starts.

"They're moving in less than two weeks!" interrupts Lucy. "Did she tell you that part?"

Tally's mouth clamps shut. *Two weeks?* She shuffles her feet and stares at the ground, not wanting any of them to see her face.

"Tally?" Layla's voice is gentle. "Are you OK? Lucy thought it'd be really exciting to tell you when we were all together but I should have told you first. I'm sorry."

Tally closes her eyes. She doesn't want to make Layla feel bad, just because her heart is breaking. She needs to tell Layla that it's all fine – she owes it to her to do that, no matter how hard it is to find the words.

Opening her eyes, she takes a big breath and stretches her mouth into something that she hopes looks like a smile.

"I think that it—" she tries again, but it's too late. Lucy and Ayesha have pulled Layla away, words pouring from their mouths like they just come for free and don't demand any effort.

"It's an amazing opportunity and you totally shouldn't feel bad!" gushes Ayesha.

"We can FaceTime you loads!" Lucy glances over her shoulder to look at Tally. "And she'll be fine, don't worry. She won't sulk for long and we'll look after her for you."

Tally's head droops as she swallows down the hurt. She isn't sulking and she doesn't need *looking after*. She just needs them to give her a chance to speak.

The bell rings and suddenly everyone is racing around, picking up bags from the ground and sprinting for the doors, yelling instructions to each other about where they're meeting at break-time. Tally stays where she is until they've all gone, her gaze on her scuffed school shoes. She knows that she has to do something; that getting a detention for being late is the last thing she can cope with right now, but her body feels like it's been bewitched by a wicked spirit and she just can't move.

"It'll be OK, you know."

Not *everyone* has gone. Layla has stayed behind and her hand on Tally's arm breaks the evil spell.

"I think that it sounds really good for you," Tally tells her, finally able to free her voice. "But I'm going to miss you."

Layla's eyes mist with tears and she pulls Tally into a hug. "I'm going to miss you too," she says. "I bet there won't be anyone as amazing as you in Florida."

Tally gives her a quick squeeze back and then hoists her rucksack on to one shoulder.

"Probably not," she agrees.

They walk together through the now-empty school yard and are almost at the main doors when Layla pauses, looking at Tally with serious eyes.

"You need to make it work with Lucy and Ayesha and

the rest of them," she says. "Year eight is too hard to do on your own, Tally. It'll be better to hang out with them than be a loner, won't it?"

Tally nods and pulls open the door. It's true that the thought of making it through the rest of the year without *anyone* is totally impossible.

But if Lucy, Ayesha and Jasmine are her only salvation, then it's not looking very hopeful.

CHAPTER 4

Cat Appreciation Group Chat

Tally: hey, is anyone there?

Jade: hi tally – I'm here

Gory: and me. how you doing?

Tally: bad day. You?

Gory: amazing! I made a huge leap forward in the search for water on other planets and then I won a race in my porsche and after that I invented a new and unique meal.

Tally: so you watched videos on YouTube, played on your Xbox and put something gross on a piece of toast?

Gory: busted! except I put a piece of bread between 2 pieces of toast and made a bread sandwich toastie and it was delicious, thanks very much.

Jade: mine was ok. sorry that yours wasn't tally ☹
want to talk about it?

Tally: no

Jade: ok. How about I send you a photo of my cat
then? she's looking really cute today.

Tally: layla is moving to america

Jade: oh tally, I'm so sorry

Gory: that sucks

Tally: I don't know what I'm going to do. she says
that I should stick with Lucy and the others.

Gory: you said the other day that you hate hanging
out with that group though

Jade: maybe this is your chance to find other people

Gory: yeah – maybe some nicer people?

Jade: isn't there anyone at your school who's nice?
What about aleksandra – she seemed lovely when we
met her at camp last year?

Tally: ...

Jade: tally?

Gory: I liked Aleksandra – she was funny

Tally: we don't really talk any more

Jade: oh. well there must be someone?

Tally: no. but that's ok cos I can just hang out on my
own and do my own thing. that'll be ok, won't it? it's

what both of you do.

Gory: I mean, it's what we used to do, sure

Jade: since the camping trip we've kind of hung out together

Gory: it's great! nobody bothers hassling you when there's more than one of you.

Tally: oh

Jade: but you're going to be fine, tally. honestly.

Gory: you definitely will. you can totally handle layla moving away.

Jade: you're braver than anyone I've ever met

Tally: I'm not brave. I just don't have a choice.

Today's Newsflash

Layla, my best friend in the whole wide world, is leaving the school. I haven't had time to process or even think about how I will cope without having someone to hug in the morning without feeling self-conscious, or to help me with my maths or to show me where something is around the school. It's not something I'm ready to come to terms with yet, well, at least not mentally. I am writing a song about it, though, which usually helps me accept things. One of the lines in my new song is:

People come and go, but memories stay for ever,
If they are right they will come back, so never say
never.

I'm sort of relating to the famous quote I've always loved: "If you love something let it go, if it loves you it will return, if it doesn't then it was never yours."

Thinking about stress
Mrs Jarman once taught me this idea of thinking about all my stresses filling a bucket and eventually overflowing. But today on the way home, my Nike

backpack felt so heavy that it made me come up with a new idea. Ladies and gentlemen, boys and girls, welcome to the **BACKPACK OF PAIN.**

The backpack of pain starts off as a cool new backpack on your back, all light and empty. But it gradually starts filling up throughout the day and some days I wake up with it already full. What fills it? Everything that causes me stress. This might be anything from too many demands placed on me, to loud noises or really strong smells. When my backpack gets full, it really, really weighs me down, and if I don't find a way to empty some things out of it, I can collapse under the weight of it all. On some days my backpack feels really small and tight and so it gets full really quickly. This happens on days when I've not slept much, or when a horrible situation has been going on for a long time, and on other days it feels like it's been stretched bigger and I can fit more in without it feeling too heavy. Things that stretch my backpack are when I'm not feeling under much pressure – like when I'm on holiday, and there aren't many demands on me. At those times, things that would immediately cause me stress, like an itchy top, or a food I'm not mad keen on, suddenly don't seem to matter nearly so much. I can tolerate more at those times.

Ten things that help me empty my backpack when it gets too heavy for me

1. Talking to friends like Layla or Jade or Gory. They always make me feel better.

2. Writing and playing songs – it gets all my bad feelings out.

3. Hanging out with animals – dogs and horses especially. They are so non-judgy and accepting and they don't pretend to be something they're not.

4. Watching soothing videos on my iPad. Recommendations below.

5. Doing something mindful, like doodling or sewing or a jigsaw.

6. Writing down what I'm feeling, and then trying to turn it into positive self-talk. When I

was worried this week about going to school, I wrote myself a note and left it by my bed so I could read it when I woke up the next day: I am bold, I am brave, I can beat this.

7. Focusing on looking forward to nice things that are happening, or thinking back about things that have made me happy in the past, such as special days.

8. Treating myself to something that feels like I'm being kind to myself, like a long, bubbly bath with hot chocolate and listening to Taylor Swift.

9. Being around nature. Taking Rupert for even a ten-minute walk in the park can help. If I'm really trying to stop thinking about worries I ask myself to focus on what I can see, hear and smell while I'm walking.

10. Doing something really familiar that brings back nice memories and makes me feel comfortable. This could be cuddling Billy, my favourite teddy, or rewatching a movie or TV show that I loved when I was a kid.

My top five types of relaxing videos

1. Calming ones like guided meditations to the sounds of the sea. These help me focus on positive words instead of my worries.

2. Satisfying ones like someone playing with slime or peeling glue off their hands or cutting wood with a special machine.

3. Informative ones with quiet but interesting voices like David Attenborough's wildlife programmes. (I fast-forward any animal-dying parts.)

4. Sensory ones. My dad introduced me to a really old programme he used to watch as a child – it has a man called Bob with loads of hair who does paintings with a scrapy knife and a scratchy brush, who speaks in a really nice way, gentle but enthusiastic and friendly. He turns blobs of paint into amazing mountains and trees. That one appeals to all my senses so much!

5. Funny ones. I can watch dogs looking at themselves in mirrors or a cat saying, "Oh, Long Johnson," for hours! They are adorable and lift my heart.

CHAPTER 5

"I hate you!" Tally's scream echoes off the walls of the kitchen and into Dad's face, which is as screwed up and frustrated as her own. "Just leave me alone!"

"What on *earth* is going on?" Mum dashes into the room, a paintbrush in her hand. "Kevin?"

Dad wipes his hands across his face as if he's hoping to erase the scene in front of him.

"I have no idea," he tells Mum, looking at Tally in bewilderment. "I asked her if she'd like me to make her a sandwich for a snack and this is the reaction I got. She's being completely ridiculous."

Tally opens her mouth and roars, but it's less the roar of anger and more the roar of somebody in great pain.

Not that Dad can tell the difference.

"Tally." Mum puts the paintbrush down on the table

and Tally watches as a splodge of red paint drips on to the surface. "Tell me what the problem is."

Tally points at Dad, her hand shaking. "*He* is the problem," she wails. "He didn't just *ask* me – it's the way that he said it. And I am *not* ridiculous!"

"Come on," Mum says gently. "Let's sit down and talk about it. What's this really about, hey? Was school hard today? Are you feeling worried about Layla moving away?"

Tally glares at her. "This hasn't got *anything* to do with school. Or Layla."

It's not true, but trying to find the right words to tell them just how wrong everything is at school is an impossibility. She's been masking as much as she can for the last few days, in an attempt not to show how hurt she is that Layla is leaving and how scared she is at the thought of being alone and now she's got nothing left. She's an empty husk and Dad should *not* have snapped at her like that, just because she didn't hear him the first few times he asked her the question.

Mum and Dad pull out some chairs, but Tally remains standing. If she's sitting down then she's trapped, and when she feels like this she really needs to be on her feet and ready to run.

"Is this really all about a sandwich?" asks Dad. "Because you could have just said: *no, thank you*, and asked for something else. It's basic manners and it costs nothing."

"Shut up!" bellows Tally. "Just stop yelling at me, OK?"

Dad blinks. "I'm not yelling," he says, looking at Mum. "Am I?"

"No, you're not," she tells him, giving him a reassuring look. "But this line of conversation isn't helping."

Dad shakes his head, his shoulders drooping slightly. "I don't know what I'm doing wrong," he murmurs. "I just can't seem to get it right with her, no matter what I say. I thought we were getting somewhere yet everything seems to be kicking off again."

Mum reaches across the table and puts her hand on his. "You're doing fine," she tells him. "Remember what they told us – it's not a journey on a straight path and there are going to be lots of twists and turns as she gets older."

"I'm standing *right here*," Tally shouts at them. Why do people constantly think it's fine to talk about her as if she can't hear them? It's bad enough that it happens at school but to have her own parents act like she isn't even in the room is a step too far. "And I'm not an *it* or a *her* or a *she* – I'm me. It's incredibly rude to discuss me like I'm not here!"

"We know that," soothes Mum. "Why don't you go and chill out in your room for a bit and we can talk about this when we're all feeling a bit calmer?"

"I *am* calm!" The words screech around the room. "It's *you* who isn't calm. Why don't you send yourselves away instead?"

"That's a tempting suggestion," mutters Dad. Mum makes a funny noise and then clamps her hand across her lips as if she's trying to hold back the sound. Not that it helps – Tally can see the small smile at the edge of her mouth.

"Don't laugh at me," she warns.

"I'm not laughing," Mum assures her. "It's just that you telling us how calm you are in a screaming voice made me think about other things people might say in a contradictory way."

"Do you mean something like this?" Dad pulls a sad face. "I am super happy."

Mum nods. "Exactly. Or maybe this." She yawns exaggeratedly. "I am so full of energy right now."

"I'm really bored," says Dad in an eager voice.

"I'm miserable," sings Mum, waving her hands in the air and getting up to skip round the kitchen. She looks so daft that Tally can't help but give a small smile of her own.

"People do that all the time, though," she tells them, finally slumping into a chair. "They say one thing with their words and another thing with their faces."

"That's true," agrees Mum, stopping her skipping.

"So how can we work out what the truth is?" Tally frowns. "If nobody says what they really mean?"

"Well." Dad leans forward and takes one of Tally's hands. "I think we have to listen a bit harder and really pay attention to what the person *isn't* telling us, as well as listening to the things that they *are* saying."

Tally pauses and thinks about what he's just said. It makes sense but it sounds like a lot of extra work and maybe it would be a whole lot easier if instead of pretending everything was fine, people were a bit more honest.

"It wasn't about the sandwich," she whispers. "Well, it was a bit. But it was about other stuff too. School and Layla and *everything*."

Dad nods, as if he knew that all along.

"How can we make it better?" asks Mum, picking up

Tally's other hand. "What can we do to help?"

"Not make me go to school," says Tally and they both squeeze her hands and start talking about how this won't last for ever and things will all work out and how everyone finds school tricky at some point or another. They tell her that they'll talk to Mrs Jarman again about making sure the teachers let her use the Safe Space and maybe it's time for another meeting with the deputy head to discuss a few new strategies and she zones out and lets them speak because it's making them feel better at least.

Even if none of what they are saying is going to make the slightest bit of difference to how safe she feels in school.

CHAPTER 6

The noise bounces off the walls of the school canteen and into Tally's ears. She grits her teeth and leans closer to Layla, trying to block out everything except the sound of her best friend's voice.

"I can't believe I've only got a few more days left," Layla is telling Lucy. "I really wanted to go shopping with you all one last time but we're staying with my gran on the way to the airport and Mum wants us to have the whole weekend with her."

Lucy pulls a sad face. "We're going to miss you loads."

Ayesha nods. "It's going to be so weird not having you there," she tells Layla. "It won't be the same just being the three of us."

Lucy laughs and knocks Ayesha with her elbow. "Your maths is rubbish. There'll be four of us, won't there?

Me, you, Jasmine – and Tally." She turns to Tally. "You asked your mum, yeah? You're definitely coming?"

It would be the easiest thing in the world to tell Lucy that she's asked her mum but they already have plans for the weekend. Or maybe she could say that she's forgotten to ask and she'll check later after school and then "forget" again. Tally opens her mouth but Layla gets there before her.

"She'd love to come," she states. "Right, Tally?"

Tally closes her mouth and stares at Layla. Why would she say that when she knows that Tally has never once gone into town with them all and that shopping is her least favourite thing to do?

"We should place bets on whether she actually turns up," says Ayesha, ripping open a packet of crisps.

Jasmine nods. "My money is on her saying that she'll come but then cancelling at the last minute, like she does every single time we invite her anywhere."

Lucy snorts. "How long has it been since she came out with us? It's got to be more than a year, yeah?"

Tally's skin prickles. They're talking as if she isn't standing right here, listening to every word. Last time she checked, she wasn't invisible – which means they can see her. They just don't think she's that important.

"It'll be fun," Layla tells her quietly. "You should try to do more stuff with them once I've left and it might cheer you up after we've said goodbye on Friday."

Tally knows that nothing can possibly make her feel OK about Layla leaving but she also knows that if she stays at home then she'll spend the entire weekend wondering what they're doing without her and whether they're talking about her. And next Monday will be awful because they'll have loads of inside jokes and conversations that she won't understand and, honestly, maybe it would just be easier to go along with it and deal with the horror of a shopping trip.

Perhaps it *will* help her cope with the awfulness of saying goodbye to her best friend.

Ignoring the dark, writhing tendrils of fear that are squirming inside her head, Tally takes a deep breath and smiles at Lucy.

"I can come shopping," she says. "I'm really looking forward to it."

"Brilliant!" Lucy beams at her and Tally slumps back into her chair. She did it. She said the right words.

That wasn't so hard.

"What a waste of a Saturday," says Luke, craning around Ameet, who is sitting next to him. "You should come to the football with us – it's always a right laugh and way better than shopping."

Tally looks down at the table. Things have been OK between her and Luke for a while now, but since they started year eight and they've all been hanging out together in a big group, she still feels a bit awkward around him and Ameet. Although she'd far rather go to watch football than hang around the shopping centre, even if there's no way that she could ever admit that.

"Have you guys seen the new girl?" asks Ayesha, staring over Tally's shoulder. "She looks dope. We should get her to join us."

Before anyone can stop her, Ayesha is standing up and waving her arm in the air. "Hey! There's a spare seat over here!" She waves again and then hisses at Tally.

"Shift across a bit and let her sit down."

There isn't a spare seat but Tally moves anyway, perching precariously on the end of the bench, at risk of toppling off at any moment. Then a long pair of legs step over the bench and Tally quickly looks down at her lunchbox, not wanting to have to deal with an unknown person right now, when everything is already such a lot.

"Thanks," the new girl says. "For a minute there I

thought I was going to have to eat my lunch sitting on the floor."

Ayesha laughs. "You can sit with us any time you like," she tells the girl. "I'm Ayesha and this is Lucy and Layla." She points further along the table. "That's Jasmine, and over there are Luke and Ameet. They're not too bad, considering."

"Hey," objects Luke. "Considering what?"

"I *love* your hair," Lucy tells the new girl. "I can't believe Mr Kennedy hasn't had a go at you for that yet, though. He's on a proper power play now he's Deputy Head."

Tally peeks sideways, trying to look without being too obvious but when she catches sight of the girl sitting beside her, she forgets to be subtle and stares, her eyes wide.

"Hi," the girl says to her. "I'm Annie."

Tally says nothing, her gaze firmly fixed on the sight before her.

"Oh yeah, and that's Tally," adds Ayesha. "You'll figure her out eventually if you hang around with us."

Tally blinks and looks away, her face flushing red. Lately, Ayesha has been doing this more and more often, and Tally doesn't know what to do about it. Part of her wants to think that Ayesha doesn't mean anything by it when she says this kind of thing, but another, louder part of Tally, suspects that Ayesha knows exactly what she's doing. Although, sometimes Layla will call her on it and then Ayesha seems so surprised and upset that anything she's said might be seen as offensive that Tally knows the best thing to do is just let it go, however much the words poke and stab.

Right now, though, Layla is engaged in an animated conversation with Luke and Jasmine about her new school in Florida, and Ayesha is distracted by Lucy showing her a new beauty video on her phone, and it's just her and the new girl sitting in silence at the table.

Tally has almost plucked up the courage to speak when there is a crash as someone drops their lunch tray, followed by a cheer that echoes around the canteen. The noise builds, louder and louder, and Tally clasps her hands over her ears, trying to stop it from swamping her. Her mouth hums her favourite song and she bends closer to the table, trying not to let it all overwhelm her because a sensory meltdown in the middle of the entire school is not what she needs right now.

Across the table, Lucy's phone shifts in her hands and Ayesha smirks.

"Hey, are you OK?"

When Tally finally raises her head, she sees the new girl looking at her with concern in her eyes.

"I'm fine," she lies, because even though it's going to make her feel bad, it's better than the consequence of telling the truth. She can't even remember this girl's name so she's hardly going to answer her honestly and tell her that, actually, no, she isn't OK and what she really needs right now is to go somewhere quiet and let her head recover.

"You're Tally, right?" The girl isn't giving up. "Why did she say that I'd *figure you out*?" She jerks her head towards Ayesha, whose head is now bent next to Lucy's as they laugh at something on Lucy's phone. "What about you needs *figuring*?"

Tally shrugs. "I don't know."

The lies are certainly racking up this lunchtime.

The new girl looks thoughtful. "Well, it makes you sound mysterious, and I like that. People who need to be figured out are always more interesting than people who have every part of them on show."

"Your hair looks like a unicorn," blurts out Tally, unable to stop herself, although the howl of laughter from the other side of the table makes her regret her impulsive comment almost immediately.

"It's called balayage, *actually*," declares Lucy in a snooty voice, rolling her eyes dramatically.

"Sorry about her," adds Ayesha, looking at Annie. "She sometimes just says stuff without really thinking about it."

Tally's face flushes deep red and her leg starts to jiggle up and down. She longs to tell Ayesha to shut up but she knows that if she opens her mouth, it'll all come out wrong, as usual.

"Don't do that." Annie shoots a firm look at Ayesha before standing up and stepping back over the bench. "Tally is supposed to be your friend and you don't apologize for your friends. And, anyway, she's right. I *have* got unicorn hair."

She picks up her lunch tray and flicks Tally another look. "Catch up with you later."

And then she is gone, leaving Lucy and Ayesha with open mouths and Tally wondering what on earth just happened.

"She. Is. Amazing," breathes Lucy, gazing after her.

"What was all that about?" asks Layla, shifting closer to Tally. "What's the new girl like?"

"She's totally kick-ass," declares Lucy. "Did you hear

the way she told off Ayesha for apologizing on Tally's behalf? Honest to god, that's the kind of loyalty I want in a friend."

"She's not *that* great," huffs Ayesha. "And I was only trying to make sure that Tally hadn't offended her with that stupid unicorn comment."

"Whatever." Lucy flicks her hair over one shoulder. "Anyone with that kind of attitude, plus that level of style, is someone I'm interested in getting to know."

"Maybe she'll come on your YouTube channel?" calls Jasmine. "You could do a whole tutorial on how to dye your hair at home."

Lucy snaps her fingers. "That is an *excellent* idea," she says, standing and pulling Ayesha up next to her. "Come on. Let's go and find her and make sure that she isn't getting in with any other group."

The table empties as Ayesha and Jasmine follow Lucy as she prowls out of the canteen, intent on snagging Annie before a rival friendship gang can lay claim to her.

"Well, that was eventful!" Layla gathers up the remains of her lunch. "Do you want to head out on to the field for the last twenty minutes before the bell goes?"

Tally doesn't reply. Her head is filled with images of

a wild unicorn with rainbow hair galloping through the school hallways, chased by girls who want to capture her but can never quite catch her up.

CHAPTER 7

Cat Appreciation Group Chat

Tally: hey

Gory: hey

Jade: hi guys. so how was today?

Tally: I agreed to go to shopping in town with Lucy and the others

Gory: why did you do that?

Jade: you hate shopping

Tally: I know! but they were going on about how I never do anything and how I probably won't bother to turn up even if I say I'm going and it just felt like I didn't have a choice.

Jade: maybe it'll be ok

Tally: exactly! And lucy really wants me to go so that's good, right?

Gory: only if she's had a personality transplant

Jade: gory!

Tally: no, he's right. there's no way I can go.

Gory: just tell them you've changed your mind

Jade: yeah – maybe explain why you find shopping tricky. I'm sure they'll understand if you tell them about the bright lights and the noise and the crowds.

Gory: ☹

Tally: I can tell them but they won't listen

Gory: do you want to see a photo of hulk being not very cat-like? he's sitting on my knee and trying to lick my hand.

Jade: yes!

Tally: there's a new girl called annie. she seems maybe ok but a bit scary.

Jade: ooh, a new girl! maybe you could be friends with her?

Gory: why is she scary?

Tally: she's got rainbow coloured hair, like a unicorn

Jade: so what's scary about that?

Tally: she's being different ON PURPOSE, like it's not a thing. like she doesn't care about being stared at wherever she goes.

Jade: *shudders* that is quite frightening

Gory: do tigers and unicorns get on?

Tally: what?

Gory: well, you're a tiger girl and she's a unicorn girl and I just wondered if you could form a group or if you'd hunt each other as prey?

Tally: I don't think I'm a tiger girl any more

Jade: you are, tally! you'll always be a tiger girl.

Tally: there isn't any place for tigers at kingswood academy, I know that. lucy would definitely go on a hunting safari.

Gory: good job you aren't interested in hanging out with her then, isn't it!

Tally: it's not that easy, gory. you don't get it. now show us a cute picture of hulk.

CHAPTER 8

"I'm not going to school." Tally's head is hidden under the pillow but that doesn't mean she can't hear Mum's sigh, which just makes her heart beat even faster.

"Come *on*, Tally," says Mum, peeling back the corner of the pillow. "If you get up now then there's still time for breakfast before you need to leave."

"I'm not going."

The bed dips as Mum sits down beside her. "Let's not do this today, hey? You felt like this yesterday too, remember – but it was all OK when you got to school, wasn't it?"

Tally yanks the pillow off her face and stares at Mum in disbelief. *All OK?* How can she even begin to think that? It's like Mum hasn't got the first idea of how hard it was for Tally yesterday. It's bad enough on a normal day, with the constant noise from the other kids and the barked demands from teachers and the not knowing what's going to be thrown at her next. But these are not even normal days, not when everyone has been excitedly counting down the time until Layla gets on an aeroplane and leaves for ever. And now it's finally Friday and after today, nothing will ever be normal again. Tally is exhausted from the effort of trying to look happy for her friend while hiding her utter terror at being left behind.

"I'm ill," she states, moving her hands down to clutch her stomach. "I think I'm going to be sick."

Mum sighs again. "We both know that you're not ill, Tally. Now come on, let's get you up and dressed and then I'll make you some toast."

Tally shakes her head. There's a noise out on the landing and Dad sticks his head around the door.

"Are you not up yet?" he asks Tally, stating the obvious. "Come on, love, I've got a meeting first thing. I haven't got time for this again today."

Mum waves her hand at him. "Just go. It's all OK – I'm dealing with it."

Dad frowns. "Aren't you heading into the gallery this morning? I thought you were taking your new paintings?"

There's a pause and then Mum nods. "I'll reschedule," she tells him. "It's fine."

Dad steps into the room.

"You need to get going," he says to Mum. "Come on, Tally. You and me can rustle up some pancakes for breakfast."

"I'm sick," Tally informs him. "Everything hurts."

The second part isn't a lie.

"Pancakes will make you feel better." Dad's voice is upbeat and perky, like he's hosting a kid's television show. "Up you get – let's seize the day and all that!"

He approaches the bed and Mum stands up, shaking her head.

"Good luck," she tells him. "It's a go-slow kind of morning."

Good luck. Like she's a problem and the only way to solve her is to cross your fingers or find a four-leaf clover or rub a lucky penny.

"It's fine," Dad assures Mum. "You dealt with this yesterday so it's my turn today. I've got this – you can go and get ready for work." He gives Tally a big smile. "Come on, Tally. *Nobody* likes getting out of bed in the mornings, but it'll all be fine once you're up and dressed!"

He doesn't know what it's like to be her. She understands that and she knows that it isn't his fault that he can't see inside her head, but that doesn't make it any less frustrating or upsetting. Dad is acting like she just wants to hit the snooze button on her alarm and have an extra ten minutes in bed when the truth is that she needs to hit the snooze button on the entire day. Trying to jolly her along is the worst thing he could be doing right now.

She closes her eyes and lies very, very still, hoping that maybe he'll get bored and go away. Maybe if she lies here long enough then he'll think she's dead and go off to work.

"Tally." He bends over her bed. "I really need you to get up and put your uniform on. You have to go to school, honey. It's the law and Mum and I will get into a lot of trouble if you refuse to go in. We need you to do the right thing, OK?"

Tally's fingers dig into the mattress. She isn't *refusing* to go to school, why can't he see this isn't a choice for her? She doesn't *want* to feel like this. It must be wonderful to wake up in the morning and feel excited about the day ahead, but she literally *cannot* go to school today. Not if she wants to stay safe.

"I *can't*," she whispers. "Please don't make me."

"You can," says Dad, resting a hand on her arm. "Let's get your uniform on and I'll drive you and Nell in, how about that?"

If you make me go to school then it is going to break me into little pieces.

The words stay inside Tally's head but it feels like she's screaming them as loudly as she can. Not that anyone is listening. Or maybe they can hear her but they don't care. Perhaps everyone would prefer for her to go to school and be broken, than to stay at home and in one piece?

"I hate school," she mumbles, opening her eyes. "I'm not going in."

"Maybe we can think of something nice for you to look forward to," says Mum, pausing in the doorway. "What would you like to do when you get home?"

Tally sighs. She hasn't got the energy to keep fighting them, not today. She didn't realize that until now.

"Maybe go to the cafe and get a hot chocolate?" she says quietly.

Mum nods her head in agreement and comes back over to the bed. "It's a deal," she says. "You go to school and Dad and I will take you out to the cafe later." She grins at Tally. "If you're really lucky we might even swing for a slice of cake!"

It sounds like a bribe. Tally knows this because she heard Dad saying exactly that to Mum last week when Mum told Tally that she'd get her a new Taylor Swift T-shirt if she would get in the car and go to the dentist. It's not a bribe, though. If she's really going to have to get up and face going to school then she needs something to take her mind off it, otherwise her brain will just focus on the *bad thing* like a laser, and she won't be able to think about anything else. Which means that something is bound to go wrong, sooner rather than later. Hot chocolate is a good choice for today because there's a lot to consider. Extra-frothy cream. Marshmallows. Chocolate sprinkles. Maybe a flake stuck in the top? If she tries to focus on all of this then there's a small chance that her head will get distracted enough to let her body go through the motions of getting out of bed and ready for school.

She sits up, already so tired that it's a challenge to swing her legs off the bed. Mum reaches down for the school uniform that Tally threw on the floor last night and Dad says some stuff that she can't hear but he's smiling so presumably she's made him happy. And then

72

he dashes off to make her some breakfast and Mum eases her feet into her socks and Tally just sits there, all floppy like a jellyfish, and lets herself be dressed. She is doing what Dad told her to do, which is apparently the right thing.

But she can't help wondering who exactly decides what the *right thing* is. And what she's supposed to do if the right thing for everyone else is the absolute wrong thing for her.

By the time Tally walks through the main school entrance, she feels as if she's already lived through an entire day. The ringing bell informs her, however, that it is still only quarter to nine. Her first lesson after registration is maths and she sinks into her chair next to the window, praying that Mrs Sheridan goes easy on them today.

But the universe is clearly not listening to Tally either. Mrs Sheridan strides into the room, rubbing her hands together and giving the class a big grin.

"Good morning, 8F," she trills. "I thought we'd kickstart our day with a sure-fire way to wake you all up, so get into teams of four because it's quiz time!"

A half-hearted groan ripples around the classroom

73

and people start organizing themselves into groups. Tally sits still. She learnt a long time ago that it's far better to wait until the end when one group is short of a member than expose herself to the humiliating experience of trying to fit in to a group that clearly doesn't want her. If Layla was in this class then it would be so much better, but she's in a different set. At least they're together for all the other lessons.

Tally's heart lurches. After the weekend, they won't be together at all.

"Tally! You can join in with Luke, Jasmine and Annie," calls the teacher. "They need a fourth person."

Reluctantly, Tally makes her way across to where the other three are sitting. Annie gives her a smile and pulls out a seat next to her.

"Hi again," she says. "So – this quiz. What kind of thing is she going to throw at us?"

Tally sits down and gets out her pencil case. "Well, she usually goes over everything we've learnt this term," she tells Annie. "But the worst part is that one person from each team has to stand up for each question and shout out the answer before anyone else. We have two maths teachers, Mrs Sheridan and Mr Simpson, and they both love giving us quizzes and pretending it's *fun*."

Annie grimaces. "God, why do teachers think that putting us on the spot like that helps us to learn anything?"

"If I was a teacher I would never make kids have to speak up in class." Tally glances around the room. "I'd let them do their learning without feeling scared all the time."

"There would definitely be no pointless maths quizzes," agrees Annie. "And you'd be allowed to eat when you were hungry and go to the toilet without being made to feel like a criminal – you know, just basic human rights?'

They smile at each other and then Mrs Sheridan is ordering them to decide the running order of their teams.

"I'll go first," Luke tells them. "Because I'm the best at maths and Miss always makes the first few questions the hardest. Jasmine can go next cos she's pretty good too."

"That totally makes sense," agrees Jasmine. "Tally is useless at maths, so she definitely needs to go later. No offence, Tally."

Tally opens her mouth to object but then closes it again. What's she going to say? Like Jasmine said, she didn't mean any offence so it's probably Tally's own fault if she's feeling a bit hurt right now.

"What are you like at maths?" Luke asks, pointing at Annie. "Unless you're completely rubbish, you should go third."

Annie blinks at them both. "You're quite rude, aren't you?" she says, in a super-friendly and polite way that doesn't match her words. "I can't wait to witness your incredible mathematical intellect." She turns to Tally. "Aren't we lucky to be in a team with this pair of geniuses? Especially as *we're* both so incompetent."

"I didn't say—" starts Luke, but Mrs Sheridan interrupts him.

"The first person can stand up!" she announces.

Luke pushes himself out of his chair, casting Annie an unsure look.

"Don't worry about it," she tells him. "I'm sure you're going to be great."

"And here we go." The room falls silent and Mrs Sheridan gives them a serious look. "The rules are the same as always. A point to the first person to call out the answer, and no conferring. OK. Question one. What is ninety-eight per cent of seven pounds?"

Luke's face wrinkles in thought.

"Hurry up, Einstein," whispers Annie.

He whips round and stares at her, his eyes wide.

"You've got this!" she murmurs encouragingly. "You're the *best* at maths, aren't you?"

"No conferring at the back!" calls the teacher.

Tally watches as Luke glances anxiously between Jasmine and Annie, his lips pressed tightly together, feeling a momentary pang of sympathy towards him.

"It's six pounds and eighty-six pence!" yells a kid from another group and Mrs Sheridan claps her hands.

"Excellent," she says. "Well done! OK – the second person can stand up."

"Bad luck," says Annie, as Luke slumps into his seat. "But maybe Jasmine can make up for it, unless she gets it wrong too!" She flashes Jasmine a kind smile. "No offence, Jasmine."

Jasmine looks confused but says nothing, instead getting to her feet and steeling herself for the next question. Next to Tally, Annie leans back and raises one eyebrow.

"I can't stand braggers," she mutters. "And this school sure does seem to have a lot of them. I bet you're fine at maths when you're not being put on the spot, aren't you?"

Mrs Sheridan calls the next question and someone from another group yells out the answer. Jasmine sits down, her face flushing. Annie offers a few words of condolence and then proceeds to stand up and answer the next, and hardest, question in a matter of seconds.

"You never said that you were good at maths," says Luke as she sits down, his voice slightly accusing.

"I didn't get a chance," she replies, shrugging. "You were both too busy telling me how amazing you are."

Luke stares at her for a moment and then grins. "Fair enough. I guess we deserve that. You're definitely better than us."

Annie laughs. "It's not about being *better*. I like maths but I'm useless at English so don't pick me to be on your team in that class if you want to win, OK?"

And then it's Tally's turn. Her heart races and her skin prickles with sweat as she forces herself to stand up. Annie was right – it's not the maths that's the problem. She can do it all when she's given time to think about it, when her brain can focus on the numbers. But this, right now, has got nothing to do with testing her maths ability. This is testing her ability to cope under pressure; to ignore everything around her and think only about the question. And it's hard to do that when your brain sees and hears and notices *everything*.

Her legs shake and her head fills with cotton wool and when Mrs Sheridan starts speaking, she hears only a buzzing, like the static on an old radio.

"Are you OK?" whispers Annie.

Tally can't reply but her hands grip the edge of the table as if she's clinging on to the side of a precipice.

"You can just go to the Safe Space, you know," murmurs Luke, which is weird because Tally didn't even know that he knew the Safe Space existed, even though it was partly due to him that she needed it in the first place.

But she can't go there now because it's not going to help. Last year, in year seven, she really needed the Safe Space that Mrs Jarman, the drama teacher, set up next to the library after the situation with Luke and her tiger mask and the resulting meltdown that Tally had in front of the entire class. It was somewhere she could go when things got too much and all the teachers knew that. She would go and lie on her beanbag and watch the flickering lights and give her head time to recover from the constant effort of being in school.

But it doesn't work the same this year, not now that

she's in year eight. She's tried to go there but by the time she gets back into whichever lesson it is that she's left, she's missed too much work. And then she has to take it home and she never understands what to do because it's hard to teach yourself about energy changes in chemical reactions when you've missed the introduction *and* the practical.

And it isn't just the work that's the problem with the Safe Space. She often uses it at break-time and lunchtime, when the halls and corridors are filled with screeching kids and food being flung about, and there's nowhere to hide. But the other week, when she came back to the field for the last ten minutes of lunchtime after spending the rest of the time chilling out in peace, she didn't have a clue what anyone was talking about. And when she tried to join in, nobody except Layla could even hear her and it felt like she was intruding.

It was horrible; even worse than coping with all the noise.

But the biggest problem of all is that while time stands still for her when she is in the Safe Space, it keeps on moving for everyone else and there is just too much to catch up with when she finally emerges. The best Safe Space of all would make the outside world stop moving forward and freeze in time, just for a few minutes, so that Tally can breathe properly and tape her broken parts back together – but not even lovely Mrs Jarman can make that happen.

The triumphant cry of someone yelling the answer brings her back to reality and Tally sits down, her legs heavy with relief that her ordeal is over and her heart even heavier with the sudden knowledge of what she must do.

There's a reason that animals group together. It makes it easier to keep warm. Hunt prey. Get information. Stay safe. And Tally is tired and cold and terrified at the thought of having to fend off predators all by herself once Layla leaves. She knows now that she was wrong when she told Gory and Jade that she didn't have a choice. It's just that she needs to choose between two impossible options.

Go her own way and be unheard, unseen, unknown.

Or do whatever it takes to be accepted by the other girls.

No more swimming on the edges. No more joining in only when she feels like it. No more going to her Safe Space or anything else that reminds people of how different she is. Because animals only bond with other animals who look and sound and think like them.

And being alone is not an option.

Not if she wants to survive.

Today's In-Depth Report:
School Anxiety Part 1

Some people call this "school refusal". Personally, I do not like that term as it makes me feel like I'm being accused of making a choice to not want to go to school, which of course is not the case. When it's at its worst, my brain and body actually go into shutdown and don't allow me to leave the house, or even my bed in some cases. So of course it's not a choice in any way, because who would *choose* that?

Some days when Mum or Dad try to shift me from my bed with chivvying, or promises, or threats, I feel like a limpet stuck to a rock. No matter how hard you try to pull a limpet off a rock, you will never do it. Sometimes you get a tiny bit of movement and for a second you think the limpet is going to give up and let go but all you have done is ensure they are stuck even harder. And what you don't see is the damage you are doing to the limpet under the shell. All that standing firm against predators takes its toll on the limpet's strength. But the limpet's brain is wired so that it can't give in even if it wants to. Why? To protect itself from danger and possible death.

I know, I know, school does not = danger and possible death. But try telling that to my brain when I'm in panic mode. How can that be good for me?

Why do I have to go to school?

Sometimes it feels like me walking through the school door is more important to my teachers and parents than any torment going on in my brain. Like they want me there at all costs – propped up and going through the motions, even though I'm too anxious to take in anything and learn. As long as they can tick that register to say that I'm in, they feel they have achieved their goal.

Usually, if I can possibly do it, I go through the motions of getting dressed and getting in the car like a zombie. But sometimes the wave of panic hits me as I open the car door to get out. And then I will do everything I can to avoid the situation. It reminds me of Rupert when I took him past a butcher's the other day. For some reason he got totally freaked out by the carcasses hanging in the window. He would not go past and went into total panic mode, straining backwards on his lead then throwing himself over, twisting and turning. No way was he walking past that window. He pulled back so hard he slipped out of his harness – luckily I managed to catch him before he ran into the road. But I realized that if I was going to keep him safe I needed to listen to him next time, try to understand him and not force him to do something that was clearly not OK for him.

Sometimes I go to bed feeling OK about going to school the next day. Then it's as if my brain makes a decision while I'm asleep about whether I'm able to face school or not.

When I wake up in the morning and know it's one of THOSE days where I can't go in, I feel a cloud of guilt consume me. While I'm waiting for my mum to ask how I'm doing, I don't always know whether I'm going to reply, "Yeah, I'm fine!" or just keep quiet.

Of course I wish I wasn't like this. I dream about the days when I can be excited for school or, if not actually excited, then at least able to go in. The hard part is not feeling believed, though – or being told I'm just not trying hard enough. I wish people would help me and listen instead of accusing me.

CHAPTER 9

Cat Appreciation Group Chat

Jade: hi you guys! I'm so glad it's finally friday! what are you both up to?

Gory: not much. mostly playing on my Xbox & trying to avoid being dragged out on a walk with my mum.

Tally: I had to say goodbye to layla after school

Jade: oh tally, i'm so sorry. that must have been really hard.

Gory: saying goodbye is horrible

Tally: I don't want to think about it

Jade: have you got any plans for the weekend?

Tally: I'm going shopping in town tomorrow. lucy invited me to go with them all, remember?

Gory: I thought you were going to cancel? why are you still going? I bet their shopping trip is going to be as horrific as they are.

Jade: that's not very nice, gory

Gory: they aren't very nice

Jade: true

Tally: they're not that bad, you guys

Gory: yeah right. so it wasn't lucy and ayesha who told everyone that your dog only has 3 legs & then every time you walked into a room you had to deal with kids hopping around, pretending to be rupert?

Tally: I don't know why I even told you about that. it was fine. he's just a stupid dog and he does only have 3 legs.

Jade: tally! you can't say that – you love rupert ☺

Gory: fine? are you serious? they made you cry & you ended up hiding in the toilets. you're always telling us how awful they are.

Tally: …

Jade: tally?

Gory: and wasn't it lucy who put that note in your bag, pretending that it was from ameet asking you out on a date?

Tally: …

Jade: that's enough, gory. tally knows them better than we do and if she wants to go shopping with them then we should support her.

Gory: thank god cos if I had to go to kingswood academy & get to know them any better then I'd be totally miserable. I don't know why you didn't just tell her how upset you were.

Tally: it was a joke. lucy put fake notes in other people's bags too.

Gory: did anyone else believe it, though?

Tally: yes, actually. aleksandra believed it so it wasn't just me. and it was quite funny when she went up to ameet & asked him what time he was picking her up.

Jade: no wonder you and aleksandra don't talk any more

Gory: oh great. I take it all back – they are excellent friends.

Tally: get over yourself, gory. it wasn't lucy's fault that we were so gullible.

Jade: well it definitely wasn't your fault – and it wasn't a very nice thing to do to either of you, tally. maybe you should tell them that you don't like it when they do stuff like that?

Tally: they're my friends. they're not going to like me if I can't take a joke, are they?

Gory: it's not actually a joke when it makes you feel bad. and what about standing up for aleksandra? she was your friend too. She seemed really nice at camp.

Jade: can't you just talk to them? you did that last year on the trip and it worked really well.

Tally: it's different this year. nobody ever listens to me so there's no point in saying anything. and if I don't fit in then I'm going to be all on my own, especially now layla has gone.

Jade: you've got us. and we like you.

Tally: you aren't here. you don't count & it's different for you – you don't care that you don't have any friends.

Gory: ouch

Jade: she doesn't mean it like that, gory

Gory: how does she mean it then? cos she's sounding a bit like one of them right now.

Tally: you just don't get it

Jade: so tell us

Tally: what's the point? you won't understand.

Gory: I get it. you care so much about being accepted by *them* that you're letting them do whatever they want to you and anybody else.

Tally: it's called having friends, gory. not that you'd know anything about that.

Gory: apparently not

Jade: come on, guys, let's not fight ☺ if tally wants to hang out with all of them then that's her decision.

Gory: I'm not fighting. it's not me who's breaking bits off myself just so that I can fit in.

Tally: what's that supposed to mean? I'm not breaking anything.

Gory: yeah, ok. only the tally I met last year wouldn't stand by & let other people get away with being so awful. what's more important? being you & speaking up or being part of the group & staying silent?

Tally: ...

CHAPTER 10

It's suppertime before she gets her chance to ask.

"How was your day?" Dad looks at Nell, finally switching off his phone and putting it next to him on the table.

"Exhausting," she groans, completely predictably. "I've still got so much work to finish and the exams are—"

"Can I go into town with my friends?" asks Tally, her heart racing with worry that they won't agree. "Tomorrow morning?"

"Don't interrupt your sister," Dad tells her. "Carry on, Nell."

"As I was saying," says Nell, shooting Tally a snarky glance. "The exams are really—"

"But *can* I?" Tally stares at Mum.

"We'll talk about it in a minute," Mum answers calmly. "Once Nell has told us about her day then it will be your turn and we can talk about you."

Tally makes a huffing noise. "That won't be in one minute," she points out. "Nell is going to blather on about her stupid exams for *hours*, so just tell me. Can I go?"

"Tally." Dad puts his fork down on to the plate. "We're listening to Nell right now and when she has finished talking we'll discuss what it is that you want to tell us about. OK?"

"Not OK," Tally tells him, her legs starting to twitch. "I just need to know. My friends are hanging out in town and I want to go too, so can I?"

"What friends?" mutters Nell. "Those mean girls that you sit with at lunchtime are *not* your friends, Tally, and if you think that they are then you're being kind of stupid."

"I am *not* stupid!" yells Tally.

"Nell!" admonishes Mum. "That was rude and completely uncalled for. Apologize to your sister, right now, please. You know that she had to say goodbye to Layla earlier – a little kindness would be appreciated right now."

"Maybe they should *both* apologize?" Dad suggests lightly. "And then perhaps we can move on with hearing about Nell's day and *then* talk about Tally going into town at the weekend. How does that sound?"

"What do *I* have to say sorry for?" howls Tally, and now her arms are flapping and waving in the air, her body screaming her fear and frustration even louder than her voice. But Dad can't hear her. And then one of Tally's hands knocks into her glass and water floods across the table and on to Dad's phone.

"For goodness' sake!" he yells, pushing his chair back with a screech. "My phone!"

Tally freezes as he grabs for a towel and dabs at the screen.

"It was an accident," says Mum.

"I know that." He gives up with the tea towel and dashes across the kitchen to yank open the cupboard door. Tally watches as he grabs a bag of rice and pours it into a bowl and then turn and shake his head at Mum. "But if my phone is broken then it's going to cause me a major headache."

"It wasn't my fault." They aren't the words that she wants to say but the fear that Dad is going to blame her or be angry with her for trashing his phone makes it impossible to say what she's really thinking.

Nell makes a snorting noise which Tally chooses to ignore. There's enough going on without adding her irritating sister to the mix.

"I understand that it was an accident," Dad agrees, ramming the phone into the bowl of rice and staring at it sadly. "You didn't meant to spill the water, I know that. But it's still important to take responsibility for your own actions, Tally."

"You need to apologize," Mum tells her.

Silence floods the room as Tally stares at the table. She's sorry about the phone, she really is – but surely they should know that without her saying some random words? People say stuff all the time and don't really mean it – she would far rather someone *show* her that they're sorry than just fling out a few pointless words. But that's what her parents seem to think matters most.

"Sorry," she mumbles, not looking at either of them.

"Rosa dropped her phone down the toilet and it still works," Nell tells them.

"That's reassuring," says Dad.

"That's foul," shudders Mum. "I think I'd have just left it in there. Nobody wants to be using their phone after that."

Dad walks over to the table and sits back down. "I guess it rather depends on whether she had availed herself of the facilities first."

"Gross, Dad!" squeals Nell, pulling such a disgusted face that even Tally laughs a little bit.

"OK," says Mum. "So you want to go into town tomorrow with your friends?" She looks across at Dad. "I can't see a problem with that, can you?"

Dad nods. "If you really want to go then that's fine with me. I need to pop to the music shop for some more guitar strings so I can drop you off on the way."

Tally hesitates. She *doesn't* really want to. But she can't *not* go – that's not an option. And if she tries to tell Mum and Dad that she's petrified about going to the shopping centre without them or Nell but she's even more scared about having to go to school next week if she doesn't do what everyone else is doing, then they'll never agree to the trip. And maybe Layla was right. Maybe keeping busy and doing something new will distract her from the thudding pain that she gets in her heart whenever she thinks about her best friend and the fact that she's gone.

"I really want to," she says, echoing Dad's phrase. It feels like less of a lie if she hasn't used words of her own.

CHAPTER 11

"You can leave me here," Tally tells Dad, glancing anxiously around. The last thing she needs is for the others to see her being escorted into the shopping centre by her father. She'd never live it down, although the idea of having to walk inside on her own is making her legs feel like jelly. Anything could happen to her in between leaving Dad and meeting the girls. She's pretty sure that most kidnappings happen in places like this.

"Absolutely not," Dad says firmly, and Tally's shoulders sink under the double whammy of relief and shame. "I'll walk you in and we'll find the place you're meeting them. And once we see them, I'll stay back and they'll never even know I was there."

Inside, the shopping centre is heaving with people. Tally stays close to Dad as they weave their way through

97

the throngs, heading towards the doughnut stand which is where Lucy has told her to meet them. As they approach the food court, Tally's stomach writhes like it's filled with snakes. Nell took her to one side this morning and told her that she should be prepared for them not to be there; that the whole thing could be one big joke to make her feel bad. Tally isn't sure how Nell telling her this is supposed to make anything easier, but she knows her big sister was trying to be helpful, even if all she succeeded in doing was making Tally feel like she might throw up.

And then the doughnut stand comes into sight and there they are. Lucy, Ayesha and Jasmine. And standing next to them, deep in conversation, is Annie with the unicorn hair. Tally's heart leaps in her chest and she turns quickly to Dad.

"They're here!" she exclaims. "I knew Nell was talking rubbish."

Dad stares across at the girls, who haven't noticed them yet. "Are you *really* happy for me to leave you?" he checks. "I can always stay here and have a coffee so that you know I'm close by. I can head to the music shop another time."

Tally shakes her head. The idea of Dad going to the

other side of town *is* pretty worrying, but nowhere near as bad as the thought of the other girls spotting him waiting for her at the shopping centre.

"I'll be fine," she tells Dad. "Just go."

Dad presses his lips together. "OK," he agrees. "But I'll be waiting outside the main entrance at twelve thirty. You know, the doors where we came in?"

"I *know*." Tally scowls. "Now leave before they see you."

She turns and starts to head across the food court, glancing back once to ensure Dad has followed her instructions and gone back to the car. And then, ignoring everything else, she focuses on getting past the tables and chairs and prams and baskets and people, people, people and walks over to where her friends are waiting.

"You came!" squeals Ayesha, waving wildly as Tally approaches. She turns to Jasmine. "You owe me a quid!"

Jasmine grimaces. "Damn," she mutters. "I was sure she'd bottle it."

"Now Tally's *finally* here, we can do some shopping," says Lucy, looking pointedly at the clock hanging from the balcony. "Come on – I've got a long list."

She marches off with Ayesha and Jasmine on either side of her. Tally falls in behind, next to Annie.

"I thought we were meeting at ten thirty," she mutters. "I didn't think I was late. Am I late? Were we supposed to be meeting earlier?"

"I don't know," Annie tells her. "I just bumped into them a few minutes ago and they asked me to join you. And, seeing as I don't know anyone else around here, I thought I'd hang with you guys for a bit."

"Come on!" calls Lucy. "We've wasted enough time as it is. Let's have some fun."

Tally and Annie speed up and join the others, and the next hour consists of what *Lucy* calls fun, but *Tally* defines as mindlessly dull. She trails from shop to shop, watching the others try on clothes that they're not going to buy and examine make-up that costs more than Tally's entire monthly pocket money, the whole time urging her to relax and join in. Even Annie seems to enjoy dancing in and out of changing rooms, putting on one item of clothing after another while Tally slumps against the wall and pretends to be interested.

"Come on, Tally," urges Lucy, in the fourth shop that they visit. "Try on this top. It's really boring if you just *stand there*. You might as well have not bothered to come."

Tally frowns. Lucy knows she's not into this stuff. If Layla were here, she'd never pressure Tally to try on new clothes. She'd suggest that they go and look at the fish in the aquarium downstairs or get an ice cream from the cart by the entrance.

But Layla isn't here.

"Let's *both* try it on," suggests Annie. "Look – I've got it here in red but that aquamarine will look amazing with your eyes."

She smiles encouragingly at Tally and her face is so kind and open and honest that Tally relaxes for a second. She takes the top and slips into the cubicle next to Annie, pulling off her soft, comfortable T-shirt and replacing it with the top that Lucy has chosen.

"Let's see!" clamours Ayesha and, before Tally can tell her that it doesn't fit, the curtain is whisked back and they're all standing there, observing her with critical eyes.

"Perfect!" declares Lucy, hands on her hips. "I knew it would be – I've got an eye for these things."

"I love this top so much!" Annie pulls back her own curtain. "And, Tally, you look incredible!"

Tally turns to look at her reflection. She might *look* incredible, but she doesn't *feel* it. The top is scratchy and rubs against her neck and if she has to wear it for another second she might actually scream.

"Give us a twirl," demands Jasmine. "Let's see the back."

Tally grits her teeth and turns in an awkward circle, before dashing inside the cubicle again and pulling the curtain firmly closed. It isn't until the top is yanked off and thrown on the floor and her own familiar T-shirt is safely back on that she can breathe properly. She's done what they wanted and maybe now she can relax.

Back out in the shop, the girls are waiting as she and Annie emerge from the changing room. They start hanging the tried-on clothing on the unwanted rail and then Lucy leaps forward and takes the tops from their hands.

"You *have* to get these," she says. "You both looked so good in them."

Annie laughs. "Yeah, right. Have you seen how much they cost? There's no way I can afford to buy this."

She flips over the price tag and Tally peers at the number on the card. Mum gave her a bit of money for today's shopping trip, enough for a snack and a drink and maybe something small – but this horrible scratchy top costs three times what she has in her pocket.

Lucy pushes the red top into Annie's hands and then passes the other to Tally.

"Who said anything about *buying* it?" she asks softly.

Everything stops.

Tally stands very still, her eyes fixed on the frozen scene in front of her.

Lucy's eyebrows, raised in a question.

Annie's forehead, wrinkled in surprise.

Ayesha and Jasmine's mouths, turned up in a smirk.

Her own breath, held inside, while her brain whizzes through all the possible options for what is being suggested.

And then Annie laughs and the world speeds up again. People barge past them and a loud shop announcement over the tannoy system makes Tally jump and surely, surely, surely this is all just a big joke?

"You're kidding, right?" Annie smiles at Lucy.

Lucy grins back. "Nope. If you want it then you should just take it."

She isn't kidding. It's not a joke.

Annie shakes her head. "Yeah, I don't think so."

Ayesha looks pointedly at Lucy and Jasmine. "I told you she wouldn't be chill," she tells them.

Jasmine pulls a sad face. "I did *not* think you'd be chicken," she says to Annie.

"It's just a top." Lucy's voice holds a clear challenge.

"We're not suggesting you rob a bank or anything."

Annie rolls her eyes and reaches over to hang the top on the rail. "Whatever," she tells them. "I'd say it's been a pleasure, but I'd rather not lie." She glances at Tally. "Are you staying with them or do you want to come with me and get an ice cream?"

Getting away from this shop and Lucy's suggestion is all that Tally wants right now. In fact, the idea of going with Annie and getting an ice cream sounds like exactly what she needs. She opens her mouth to reply but Lucy beats her to it.

"I hope you enjoy spending time on your own," she says to Annie, her eyes narrowing. "Because nobody at Kingswood Academy is going to want to hang out with someone as lame as you." She shoots a look at Tally and delivers the punchline. "Nobody who cares about having any friends, that is."

Tally shuts her mouth and clutches the top in her hands. If she goes with Annie now, then she'll have thrown away everything she's worked so hard to get. And Lucy, Ayesha and Jasmine *are* her friends, aren't they? She might not always like what they do but that's the thing about having friends – you forgive them when they do stuff that isn't great and, in return, they look out for you. Layla warned her how tricky it would be to deal with year eight on her own and now she's been given the chance to be part of the group, she can't do anything to jeopardize her position.

"Tally?" Annie gives her a concerned look. "You don't have to stay, you know? You can make up your own mind."

But that's the problem. She doesn't know if she can, because every time she tries to make her own decision, it goes wrong. She needs the girls, no matter how much they make her head buzz with worry. She needs to be inside the group because being on the outside is just too scary.

"Don't tell Tally what to do." Lucy puts one hand on Tally's arm. "Just because you're not brave enough to take the top doesn't mean she's as pathetic as you."

"Tally is super brave," agrees Ayesha. "Aren't you?"

Tally hesitates. Jade and Gory think she's brave, or they used to anyway, and Mum is always telling her how courageous she is. They must all know something that she doesn't, because the last thing she's feeling right now is brave. But maybe she can be.

She gives a tiny nod.

"Excellent!" Lucy claps her hands. "OK, here's what

we're going to do. We'll go outside and wait for you so that it doesn't look too suspicious. And after a couple of minutes, you can hide the top under your T-shirt and follow us out. OK?"

"OK." The word has left Tally's mouth before she can stop it.

Annie looks at her disappointedly and then shrugs. "You don't have to do this," she tells her one last time. Then she's gone, stalking through the shop with stiff shoulders, pushing through the other shoppers and away.

"*Finally*," says Ayesha. "She was the most boring person I have ever met in my entire life."

"She was actually even more boring than Tally," snorts Jasmine. "No offence."

"*Shut up*," snaps Lucy. "Tally isn't boring. She's one of us and she's about to prove that." She gives Tally a quick look. "You know what to do, right? It's all good."

The three girls turn and walk away, leaving Tally smiling and nodding at their retreating backs, although her body is lying. She doesn't know what to do and none of this is good. She's never stolen anything in her life and she doesn't even know if she actually can. All she does know is that she has two choices. Put the top back on the rail and walk out of here with her conscience intact and her social life in pieces. Or shove it under her T-shirt and leave the shop with a heavy heart but her place in the group secure and safe.

As is so often the case, her choices aren't real choices at all.

Is it a RED day, an AMBER day or a GREEN day?

On a RED day, there is absolutely nothing I can do to get to school, short of my parents tying me up and transporting me on a stretcher. Actually, I'd better not give them ideas. To be honest, it feels like that's almost what happens on some days.

On an AMBER day, I really am panicky about going to school, but if I'm supported in the right way I may be able to find enough strength to just about push myself. This is a delicate balance, and at any time I could move to RED if something goes wrong, like Dad talking too much, or finding out that Layla isn't going to be in, or realizing I have a lesson like PE, which is just the worst.

On a GREEN day, even if I wake up negative, I can get into school. Don't think I'm happy about it, but I've either focused on something positive that's happening there – which is usually friendship based – or I'm feeling strong enough to put on a front. And of course when I feel that way I try and go with as little fuss as possible, because I know how much it means to Mum and Dad and I just want to make them happy for once instead of always stressed.

On GREEN days I'm pretty much masking – working hard to hide my true feelings. That's exhausting and ends up taking its toll when I get home and let my true feelings out. That's when Mum, Dad and Nell really have to watch out.

The hard thing is I won't always be able to tell my parents if it's a RED, AMBER or GREEN day. Sometimes I'm not sure myself. So they have to kind of work that out by tuning into me.

Three things parents need to know about school anxiety

1. If it's a RED day, please don't make your child feel any worse than they already do. When my parents tell or show me how stressed they are, it just makes me feel more anxious and guilty and I can't stop that coming out in anger. Then that makes me feel even worse because I start thinking that they are having a horrible life all because of me.

2. Punishments do not work! If I'm already saying I CAN'T go then threatening me with taking away my phone is not going to make me turn it all around. This

assumes I can go to school and I'm just choosing not to. I already feel terrible, but this makes it worse.

3. Bribery doesn't work either, but sometimes having something nice to look forward to does. I know it sounds like the same thing, but it's all about how it's done. If my mum says, "Don't forget after school today we are bathing Rupert," or, "I'm really excited about taking you shopping at the weekend, just three more days at school," then it might help me to focus my brain on that instead of the worry about school, and I might be able to get through. I say might because things that work one day don't always work on another.

CHAPTER 12

It's *not* a good day. It is *definitely* not a day that she can be in school, but Mum and Dad are standing firm, even though Tally knew the moment she opened her eyes that everything was wrong and too loud and too much. Even her favourite music is too much to cope with this morning, but she still slips her headphones over her ears in the hope that they will help filter out some of the turbulence in her mind.

Nell has already left by the time Mum has pulled Tally's socks on and coaxed her legs into her skirt.

"I'll drive her in," she tells Dad as she gently eases Tally down the stairs and into the kitchen. "Let's at least try to get the week off to a good start."

"I don't want to go," Tally murmurs but it is entirely possible that the words only exist in her head, because nobody responds. Mum guides her into a chair and then crouches on the floor, gently pushing a shoe on to each of Tally's feet. And quiet words flow between her and Dad without any understanding that Tally isn't listening to music and she can hear their every word and that each one is a weapon, landing blow after blow on their silent daughter.

Having rules should be helping her to cope.

Smash.

School is once again suggesting that it could be a home issue. They say that she's *anxious but able*, as if really she's totally fine but just a bit of a worrier, which Mum and Dad know isn't the case but how are they supposed to work with school if they can't see the bigger issue?

Shatter.

They can't keep letting her opt out of the stuff she finds difficult because what will happen when she gets older? What about her potential?

Flatten.

She has to go to school just like all the other kids. Doesn't she? Doesn't she? Doesn't she?

Demolish.

"It will be OK when you get there." Dad picks up his

briefcase and plants a small kiss on the top of Tally's head. "Just try to do your best, sweetheart."

If she thought that she could find the right words then she'd open her mouth and beg them to let her stay at home. But it's already taking all her energy just to stay sitting in this chair and she knows that even if she tries to talk, it won't come out right. She'll start crying or shouting or throwing stuff about, and they won't hear her fear. They'll only see her being difficult.

By the time that Mum has led her out of the kitchen, down the hallway and out to the front drive, Tally is not Tally at all. She is splintered into tiny fragments that on the outside might still look like her, but on the inside are a mess of broken parts. Mum opens the door and Tally pours her tiny pieces into the car.

Mum talks to her the entire drive to school but Tally doesn't listen. All she can think about is what they said about sticking to the rules. Tally likes rules; they keep her safe and they let her know what is expected. She's always been good with rules up until now and they're right – the rules should be helping. If she can't even stick to them then the world is suddenly an even more terrifying place.

Images of Saturday morning flood her head. The

sensation of the stolen item against her skin. The terror as she walked past the security guard, certain that he would hear her pounding heart and arrest her on the spot. The delight on Lucy's face when she pulled the spoils from beneath her T-shirt and the praise that felt warm for a second before instantly chilling. The knowledge that she had passed their test but that she had failed in every other way.

Spoils is entirely the right word for the stolen top. It has ruined everything, and even the knowledge that she shoved it inside one of the shopping centre bins before Dad collected her can't stop it from looming large in her head when she least expects it, tainting everything she does.

If the colour of rage is red, then the colour of guilt is aquamarine.

The car stops and Mum is still talking, but Tally has taken off her seat belt and crumpled her fractured pieces into the footwell where she is held tightly between the seats, her hands over her ears. Mum retreats and picks up her phone and then shortly afterwards, the car door opens and Mrs Jarman, the one teacher who seems to understand a little bit of what it's like to be Tally, is standing outside with an encouraging smile.

It's an unfair move and Mum knows it.

Tally takes her hands from her ears and pushes herself up out of the footwell, not looking at the teacher.

"There we are," says Mum, her face filled with worry. "I know it's going to be a bit strange without Layla here but Mrs Jarman is going to walk you into your tutor group and make sure you're OK."

Tally takes hold of the rucksack that Mum is passing her and levers herself out of the car, her legs tense.

"That's the way," says Mrs Jarman. "There's no rush."

"I'll see you later," calls Mum as they start to walk towards the gate. "Well done, Tally! I'm proud of you."

Tally walks stiffly beside Mrs Jarman, staring straight ahead. Mum still doesn't get it. None of them do. They think that just because she's doing what they want her to do that she must be feeling better, but that's not true. She's still broken and hurting and wrong inside.

She just can't let her teacher see that.

She must always be the good girl at school – and that's the one rule that she *can* still keep.

When school is finally over, Tally sneaks a biscuit to Rupert and after giving him a long cuddle, she heads upstairs to her bedroom. She needs a break from all the confusion and she's tired – more tired than she can ever remember being before. Even though she was with her friends all day – right in the middle of the action – she still felt as if she was getting it wrong, and it was exhausting. There are only two things that can make her feel good when she feels this way – her music and her dog. They've never let her down and they are always there, no matter how difficult everything else might be.

Turning on her keyboard, she runs her fingers over the keys, picking out the notes of a melody that has been playing in her head since Saturday morning. She often likes her music to be positive and upbeat, but today her fingers find the minor chords and she lets them wander, creating something different to her usual style. Then, once she's happy with the melody, she turns to her journal and starts to write, pouring out everything that she's feeling on to the page. And, as the words leave her body, she can feel herself becoming just a tiny bit lighter.

A tiny bit happier.

Once she's finished, she sets up the camera on her phone. She always records her songs, no matter how good or bad she thinks they are, and puts them on her YouTube channel, for an audience of just her.

Her channel is private and there's no point in making it public. Nobody ever listens to what she says in real life when she's standing right in front of them, so she knows there's no way they'd take the time to hear her online. It's fine, though, because her songs aren't *for* anyone else. And if she doesn't share them, then there's no risk of them becoming yet one more thing to be used against her.

"Tally?"

It's Mum, knocking on the door. Tally ignores her and keeps playing.

"Tally?"

The door opens and Mum walks inside, messing everything up.

"Get out!" Tally screams, spinning to face her. "I didn't say that you could come in and you've ruined my song now! You're so stupid."

Mum's face crumples and she shakes her head. "I'm sorry I interrupted your song but, Tally, it really hurts me when you speak to me that way."

Tally glares at her. "It really hurts *me* when you barge into my room! What's the point in knocking if you're just going to come in anyway, hey? Tell me that!"

Mum takes a deep breath. "I've come to tell you that

tea is on the table and we're sitting down to eat," she says, ignoring Tally's question, just like she ignored her clearly closed bedroom door. "Join us if you want to."

And then she walks away, leaving Tally to wonder why nobody else seems to understand that what she wants and what she can do are not the same thing.

CHAPTER 13

Cat Appreciation Group Chat

Gory: hey you guys – what's up?

Jade: hi gory. nothing much. what about you?

Gory: same as usual. too much homework, not enough gaming. I'm telling you, the daily grind is getting me down.

Jade: ha! except that I'm in most of your classes and I know for a fact that you haven't done any homework all term.

Gory: rude

Jade: but true

Tally: hey

Gory: tally! long time no see? long time no message? long time no hear? help me out here, jade.

Jade: it's good to chat with you, tally. how are you?

Tally: fine

Gory: steady on – don't be too enthusiastic

Jade: how was the shopping trip?

Tally: ok

Gory: was it awful? were they awful?

Tally: I said it was ok

Jade: did you buy anything nice?

Gory: did you get doughnuts? I love doughnuts.

Jade: ooh yeah – did you find any vanilla rainbow ones? they're my favourite! you could get one for the new girl at your school with the rainbow hair!

Tally: god – don't you have anything else to talk about?

Gory: here we go

Jade: tally? are you ok?

Tally: I said I'm fine. can we talk about something else please.

Gory: you don't sound fine. you sound grumpy.

Tally: you can't tell how I sound from a text, gory

Gory: I can actually

Jade: what's wrong, tally? you can tell us. was the shopping trip difficult?

Tally: what part of I don't want to talk about it do you not understand?

Gory: hey! don't be mean to jade.

Jade: it's ok

Gory: no it isn't

Tally: no it isn't. I'll just go.

Gory: you don't have to leave

Jade: don't go, tally

Tally: sorry guys. I can't do this right now.

CHAPTER 14

Nell is being super quiet this morning and hasn't moaned about her GCSEs even once, which is just as well because Tally has got bigger problems to deal with than stupid exams. She walks along the pavement behind her sister, going through her plan for the millionth time. She woke up early this morning to put part one into action and now she's reminding herself of her lines because that's exactly how her life feels right now. Like one huge theatrical production.

And she's about to give the performance of a lifetime.

The school gates are empty as she and Nell approach and Tally pauses for a second, looking up at the sky. Layla isn't here – she's four thousand miles away, with her new school and her new friends, and Tally has got to do the same. She doesn't even have Gory and Jade to talk to properly any more, so there's literally no other option than to make it work with the people who are still here – the people who could tell everyone about what she did at the shopping centre if she doesn't do whatever it takes to keep them on side. She tightens the straps on her rucksack and tries not to mind when Nell walks away without a backwards glance. She stands as tall as she possibly can. She can do this. She's rehearsed what she's going to say and she's put on her war paint – even though it took for ever and she still can't see the point.

And then she's marching through the gates and towards the wall where everyone is gathered, her heart beating like a drum.

"I can't believe that I've hit one thousand followers!" Lucy exclaims, as Tally approaches. "I'm going to celebrate later by putting up a tutorial on how to fill in your eyebrows!"

"You are *so* incredible!" gushes Ayesha. "It's like *everyone* is listening to what you have to say!"

Lucy flicks her hair over her shoulder and shrugs. "I'm just saying the things that people want to hear, I guess."

"Hi, guys," says Tally, giving them a little wave.

"You actually could have a career as a YouTuber, you know," Jasmine says, jumping down off the wall. "How amazing would that be?"

Tally looks at Lucy. "You look good today."

"*I'm* totally going to be a YouTuber," declares Ameet.

Lucy turns away from Tally and laughs. "You're going to have to sort out your own eyebrows before you can tell other people how to manage theirs!"

Ameet gives her a snotty look. "Very funny. Unlike you, I'm going to be a successful YouTuber with way more than a poxy one thousand followers. My gaming channel is going to make me millions, I know it."

"Oh, *right*." Ayesha puts her hands on her hips. "Cos people are really going to sit around and watch videos of you playing video games?"

"Yeah," adds Jasmine. "It's not exactly *thrilling*, is it?"

Luke slaps Ameet on the back and grins at the girls. "You have no idea how popular that stuff is. There's people on YouTube earning more than ten million dollars a year right now for streaming their games."

"I watched that show you were talking about the other day," says Tally. "It was really good."

It wasn't really good. It was really boring. Not that it matters, though – they aren't listening to a word she says.

She'll just have to try harder. She needs to do what Lucy does and say the things that people want to hear.

"If I had ten million dollars I'd buy a massive house with five swimming pools," Ayesha tells them.

Lucy rolls her eyes. "What's the point in that? You can only swim in one at a time. I'd have one huge pool with a diving board and a slide and tons of inflatables."

"That does sound better, actually." Jasmine jerks her head at Ayesha. "Yours was a bit lame."

"I thought the show was very interesting," Tally says, raising her voice. "Especially the part in the school."

It was not interesting. It's bad enough that she has to come to school – why anyone would choose to watch a television show about a different school is completely beyond her.

"It was *not* lame," protests Ayesha, scowling at Jasmine. "But, fine – don't expect to come over to my mansion and swim in any of my pools when I'm rich and famous."

Luke gives her a small smile and shakes his head but Tally doesn't know what he's trying to tell her. Perhaps it's that she's not really making any sound at all? Maybe she only *thinks* that she's speaking aloud but it's actually all in her head? Perhaps the reason that they aren't responding is because they genuinely can't hear her?

"La, la, la, la, la," she hums, under her breath. "Testing, testing, one, two, three."

"*What* are you doing?" asks Jasmine, because of course *now* they can hear her.

"I liked the show," Tally says quickly, going back to the beginning of her lines before they tune out of her frequency again. "It was really good."

"Are you wearing *make-up*?" asks Lucy, ignoring what Tally said and instead peering at her closely. "Actual *make-up*?"

"Oh my god, she is!" screeches Ayesha, pointing her finger in Tally's face. "That's hilarious!"

No. No. No. This is not right. It's not supposed to be hilarious.

"Amazing," states Jasmine, coming to stand next to Ayesha.

Tally swallows hard and tries to remember what she was going to say next. "I copied one of your YouTube tutorials…"

"I don't think you did," Lucy says, her mouth twitching upwards at the corners.

"I didn't know you put up a video on make-up for

clowns," says Jasmine, making Lucy and Ayesha burst out laughing.

"Give it a rest," mutters Luke but nobody listens.

Tally stands very still as Lucy steps closer, her eyes roaming over Tally's face.

"It's actually *insane* how wrong you've got it," she murmurs. "Like, did you even watch the part on applying foundation in pea-sized amounts?"

Tally nods apprehensively.

"It's totally not the right colour for your skin," Lucy tells her. "Where did you get this stuff?"

Tally tries to smile but her face feels rigid and stiff, as if all her muscles have seized up. "It's my mum's," she confesses. "I haven't got any of my own so I snuck into her bedroom and borrowed hers."

The scream of laughter from Ayesha is enough to make her want to run as fast as she can and as far away as possible. But she's determined to see this through. Running away isn't going to help make friends.

"*That's* what she reminds me of!" cries Ayesha, clutching her stomach with both hands and leaning against Jasmine for support as her body shakes with something that Tally thinks looks a lot like glee. "I was trying to figure it out."

Tally's body also starts to shake and she pins her arms to her side, desperate not to start stimming in front of the others. Sometimes her body says things that her voice cannot and her hands flap or her legs jitter up and down. Stimming helps her figure out how she's feeling and get her emotions under control but not everyone sees it like that and the last thing she wants to do now is remind them of all the ways in which she is different to them.

"What?" asks Lucy. She steps back and stares at Tally. "*What* is it that she reminds you of?"

Ayesha takes a deep breath and tries to compose herself.

"She looks like a little kid who's raided her mum's room," she snorts. "All she needs is a long, floaty dress and a pair of heels that are five sizes too big and she'll be perfect!"

"Yes!" shouts Jasmine, doubling up with hilarity. "That's *exactly* what she looks like!"

This isn't how it was supposed to be. Tally looks up again at the sky and wonders how hard she has to wish to transport herself out of here and to somewhere safe. Because whatever she's been doing so far clearly isn't working.

"You lot are ridiculous," states Luke, grabbing his rucksack and throwing it over one shoulder. "Tally looks fine to me. I can't even tell she's got any make-up on."

Lucy shoots him a hard look. "Oh, right, so you know about make-up, do you, Luke?"

"As if." He nods at Ameet. "There's still ten minutes before registration. Fancy a kick about on the courts?"

"Exactly!" Lucy calls after them, as they walk away. "So don't try giving us advice about something you know nothing about."

"Is it really that awful?" asks Tally, her voice almost a whisper.

Lucy tilts her head to one side. "I don't know when your mum last bought any make-up but I'm pretty sure this colour was discontinued about five years ago."

"And there's a reason for that," contributes Ayesha helpfully. "It's disgusting. Tell me that she doesn't put this stuff on *her* face, please?"

Tally gulps. Mum spends most of her time in her art studio and the only thing that is likely to end up on her face is actual paint, but still, the suggestion that her make-up is somehow wrong, or inferior, makes Tally's stomach flip, like she's about to throw up.

Lucy nods. "If there was any way to make it better

then I'd tell you, but the only thing you can do now is wash it all off before anyone else sees you."

"*Definitely*," agrees Jasmine.

"And don't worry about it," Lucy tells her, putting one hand on Tally's arm and giving it a gentle squeeze. "Maybe I'll put up a new tutorial called Make-up for Beginners, or something."

"Make-up for *Dummies*, more like!" sniggers Ayesha, and Lucy spins round to glare at her.

"Don't be a cow," she tells her. "We all have to start somewhere, and I seem to remember you completely messing up your eyeshadow not so long ago." She turns back to Tally. "I'll help you next time, OK?"

Tally gives her a grateful smile. "That would be good. Thank you."

Lucy bends down and picks up her bag. "You better hurry up, though. You've not got long before the bell rings and you need to get rid of it all. You don't want to bring any more attention to yourself, do you?"

Tally watches as Lucy links arms with Jasmine and saunters off in the direction of the courts, leaving Ayesha to scurry behind them. Then she lowers her head and dashes towards the side door, mortified at the idea of being seen by anyone else in year eight. Luck is finally on her side, though, and the corridors are mercifully empty. Tally races into the nearest set of toilets, her heart pounding with nerves about the apparent mess that she's made of trying to look like everyone else.

Slamming the door behind her, she tiptoes along the row of cubicles, checking that each one is unoccupied, and only when she is certain that she's alone does she dare to approach the long mirror that runs the length of the sinks. Raising her eyes, she stares at her reflection, bracing herself for the freak show that she has inadvertently become.

She leans on the sink and gets as close to the glass as she possibly can.

Her eyes.

Her cheeks.

Her lips.

Her skin.

She examines every last little bit, critically inspecting her face, looking for where she's messed up. But no matter how hard she tries, she cannot see the problem.

She doesn't think she looks like a toddler playing dress-up.

She doesn't think she looks like a clown.

In fact, she can hardly tell that she's wearing any

131

make-up and nobody at home said a word, which is surely proof that it can't be that obvious.

But the *girls* knew, and they said she'd messed it up. How is she ever supposed to get it right when she literally doesn't know how she's got it wrong?

The answer is staring her in the face. She's been looking too hard and it's right there in front of her. *She* is the problem. *She* is what is wrong and there is only one solution. Trust what Lucy told her and clean up her mistake unless she wants to be the laughing stock of the year.

Tally turns on the tap and reaches for a paper towel, letting the water soften the coarse surface before dabbing at her face. But it's not good enough. She needs to be absolutely certain that she's removed every last trace of make-up, just like Lucy said.

Because what if she leaves some evidence and everybody sees?

Grabbing a handful of paper towels, Tally rubs at her cheeks and her forehead and then around her eyes, her movements becoming more and more frantic until she is scrubbing hard, blinking back the tears that threaten to spill as the abrasive towels grate against her skin.

She was stupid to think she could be like them.

Scour and scrape.

She should have known that she'd screw up and embarrass herself.

Rasp and graze.

She'll be lucky if they're even prepared to still talk to her.

Scorch and flame.

The tears overflow but that's fine because they help wash away the last invisible residue of Mum's outdated make-up. Only when her face is red raw and she knows for sure that there is nothing left does Tally stop rubbing, looking down at the sink filled with paper towels and her pride.

And that's when the toilet door opens and they all walk in. Tally freezes but Lucy smiles at her in the mirror, a big, pleased smile that reminds Tally of a cat when it's caught a mouse.

"That's *so* much better," she says approvingly. "You look fine now."

Tally flicks her gaze back to her own reflection. Her skin looks like it's on fire and her eyes are bloodshot from all the crying.

She looks the very opposite of fine.

"It's a good job we're here to take care of you, isn't

it?" Lucy walks up behind her and pulls Tally's hair back from her flushed face. "You'd be in real trouble if we weren't around. Imagine what you'd get caught doing!"

Tally's blood turns cold. *Getting caught*. Lucy must be referring to the top that she stole, even though she promised Tally they would never mention it again.

"Your hair could actually be lush," says Ayesha, joining Lucy. "I'd love to see what it looks like when it's brushed."

Tally stiffens, but the girls are all smiling, and her head is still fizzing with worry about the make-up mistake, so she can't tell for sure if the comment about her hair is a dig or not.

"I'm good at hair," continues Ayesha. "See – I did Jasmine's French plait this morning before school and it looks really nice, doesn't it?"

Tally turns around and looks obediently at Jasmine.

"It looks really nice," she echoes, too exhausted to figure out any new words.

"I'd be happy to do yours." Ayesha strokes Tally's hair, so gently that it makes new, grateful tears spring to her eyes. "But only if you want me to."

"I'd like that," whispers Tally. "Thank you."

"Of course!" Ayesha grins at her. "You're one of us,

aren't you? We look out for each other, and nobody is going to give you any grief when you're with us. No matter what you do."

No grief … except the grief that comes from being part of this group.

No bullying … except the nagging thought that they could turn against her at any moment.

People who will watch her back … as long as she does what they tell her.

It's going to have to do.

"We'll walk you to registration," says Lucy. "Jasmine – get her bag, yeah?"

So, surrounded by the other girls, Tally is escorted out of the toilets and down the now-packed corridors. And she doesn't really know what has happened, but she feels like she does when she's sure that she's failed a test, only to discover that she's actually passed.

She's done it.

Layla has only been gone a few days and now she's one of them.

It's a terrifying thought.

Thought for the Day

For me, going to school is like a chameleon walking into a jungle. In order to not be attacked by the other animals it has to blend in, no matter how many times the setting changes.

New Song –
It Always Starts With a Smile

It always starts with a smile and nod
When you're feeling lost,
And the nod turns to a disappointing frown,
When you don't down
Their story all in one.
You wish it never happened
But you also kinda don't.
Why don't these toxic people
Come with warning notes
That somebody wrote?

And that feeling of dread,
My message is read
But there is no sign of an answer.

So my story goes on
Guess there's something wrong
With me.

CHAPTER 15

The darkness is everywhere. Tally squeezes her eyes shut tight to block it out but that only makes it worse, so she opens them again, turns on her bedside light and tries to stay calm, remembering all the things Mum has told her to do when she can't sleep.

The problem is that all the suggestions are useless. Take counting sheep, for example. Tally has tried that before and it was OK for the first few seconds, while she was imagining lovely fluffy sheep leaping over a gate and trotting off into a lush green field. But then the sheep started misbehaving and jumping back the other way and she couldn't keep track of which sheep had already been counted, because that's the thing about sheep – they all look the same.

So then she tried using the muscle relaxation

technique that someone told Mum about. She lay very still and tensed her muscles, starting with her toes and moving all the way up her body until she reached her head. But it was quite tricky trying to identify each individual muscle and she kept forgetting to do her knees so then she'd have to start all over again and after a while all she had achieved was sore legs and a wide-awake brain. Dad has suggested that she try to think of as many songs as possible that have the word "night" in the lyrics, but that just makes her brain even more awake than it was before, and then, if she thinks of a really good song, she has to get out of bed and go to find him so she can share it and make him laugh. Anyway, Dad is away for work tonight which is yet another reason she can't sleep – the house feels wrong without him here.

Mum's other idea, and this is Tally's least favourite, is to figure out what it is that's keeping her awake and then make a decision about what she's going to do about it. If it's something that she can make better right now, then she should do it – like turning on her light or pulling on her weighted blanket; but if it's something that she can't do anything about then she should try to let it go and go to sleep.

Let. It. Go.

Adults say that a lot about the things that worry or scare her and it makes Tally want to scream because, honestly, it makes zero sense. The very last thing a person should do is *let go* of whatever it is that's frightening them, because then it's out there, roaming around like a massive spider, and you can never be sure of when it might re-emerge and scuttle across your face. Far better to keep a close grip on your fears – that way they can't surprise you.

And, anyway, Tally knows *exactly* why she can't sleep and she also knows that she could one hundred per cent do something about it, if only she were allowed to. Climbing out of bed, she walks over to her door and across the landing before quietly pushing open another door and tiptoeing inside.

"Mum?"

There is no reply. The curtains are slightly ajar and, in the moonlight, Tally can see the curled-up shape of her mother, fast asleep on Dad's side of the bed.

"Mum? Are you awake?"

Tally walks closer and then reaches out to turn on the bedside lamp. There's a groan and her mum rolls over, her eyes blinking blearily in the light.

"Tally? What's wrong?"

"I can't sleep," whispers Tally. "I've tried everything, but nothing works."

Mum sighs and then peels back the duvet. "Do you want me to make you some warm milk?"

Tally shakes her head.

Mum sits up and yawns. "So what will help? You *need* to sleep, Tally. It's school in the morning."

Tally opens her mouth to tell Mum that this is exactly the reason she can't sleep, and if Mum agrees that she can stay at home tomorrow then she knows she'll be able to fall asleep in seconds. But then Mum leans forward and Tally sees her face, caught in the light from the lamp.

And she looks very, very tired.

"Are you OK?" she asks quietly.

Mum frowns, before quickly forcing her mouth into a smile. "I'm fine," she lies. "Now let's figure out how to get you some sleep. Maybe your room is too warm?"

"Why are you sleeping on this side of the bed?" Tally steps forward and puts her hand on Mum's arm. "Are you missing Dad?"

Mum gives a proper smile this time. "Maybe a little," she confesses, laughing gently.

Tally hesitates. She always gets too hot in bed and most of her cuddly toys end up on the bedroom floor by morning. Plus, she likes her space – just because she's sleeping doesn't meant that her body wants to be cramped and squished on to a tiny bit of mattress. But she's working on being different and this is her chance to show that she can put other people first.

"I'll sleep in here tonight," she tells Mum. "My room isn't right tonight."

Then she clambers on to Mum's side of the bed and lies still as Mum switches off the light and the room settles into quiet once more.

"I'm sorry that I woke you up," Tally whispers.

Mum reaches out and gives Tally's hand a quick squeeze.

"It's fine," she whispers back. "I love you, darling girl."

Tally squeezes Mum's hand back, then rolls away, trying to find a cool bit of sheet. She hasn't solved her problem of school, but at least, if she absolutely *must* go, she's got the other girls looking out for her. If only she could quieten the tiny voice in her head, then everything would be a lot easier. But it won't stop hissing in her ear that, no matter what Lucy said about her being *one of them*, she still needs to be careful.

Or asking her if being *one of them* is really what she wants.

By the time Mum's alarm rings, Tally has barely slept and when she did manage to drift off, her dreams were filled with awful visions of standing alone in the middle of the school, surrounded by pointing fingers and laughing faces, her crime known to everyone.

"I'm too tired to go to school," she moans, pulling Mum's pillow over her face.

"And *I'm* too tired to do this with you today," Mum tells her, hopping round the room in one shoe. "I've got a meeting this morning about my new art commission and you kept me awake half the night with your constant wriggling."

"I could stay here on my own," suggests Tally, removing the pillow and looking hopefully at Mum. "Then I could make you some lunch when you get back. That'd be nice, wouldn't it?"

"No." Mum raises her eyebrows. "What would be nice is you being dressed and downstairs in exactly five minutes, OK?"

She finds her other shoe and yanks it on before

spinning round to look at her daughter and issuing the fatal words. "Please, Tally. I really need you to go to school today. Dad will be back later and we can get a takeaway for a Thursday night treat, OK? But only if you're ready to leave on time."

Tally scowls. Mum wants her in school today, she gets it. But after last night and the swirling, unwelcome emotions that are gathering in Tally's head, it's going to take an awful lot of effort to make her brain focus on the takeaway and not on whatever trauma awaits her at the school gates. Mum seems to think that by offering a treat she's making it easier for Tally but it's not as simple as that and Tally has to work really hard to trick herself into half believing that a chicken tikka masala is going to miraculously make everything fine.

She's feeling grumpy and tired before she even reaches the school gates and the thought of another day trying to navigate the complex rule system of school and year eight and the girls fills her with dread. Nell is totally distracted by the thought of her upcoming exams which Tally tells herself is just *fine* with her, but the truth is a bit more complicated than that.

Tally is starting to think that the truth is *always* complicated.

Her feet are slow as she approaches the wall. Luke and Ameet are kicking a ball between them and the girls are perched on top of the wall, their legs swinging as they watch the boys and shout insults whenever one of them misses a pass. Tally braces herself, ready for whatever transgression she's inadvertently committed to be loudly pointed out to everyone.

"Here's that flappy girl I was telling you about!"

A group of year seven kids are suddenly surrounding her, jostling each other as they push to be at the front. Their voices are loud and coming from all directions, and Tally freezes, her arms twitching at her side.

"Oh – I've seen her before!" says another. "She's always being a bit weird."

Tally blinks. She wasn't expecting this from the younger kids as well as her own year group.

"Do that thing!" one of them yells. "That flappy bird thing. It's so funny!"

She grits her teeth and focuses every bit of attention on not letting her arms move, even one centimetre. This can't be happening. Not now, with everyone hanging out in the school yard, seeing her humiliation.

There is a movement to the right of her and the

year seven kids are scattered like bowling pins as Lucy, Ayesha and Jasmine barrel through them, shoving them out of the way.

"I'll show you something funny, if you like!" Lucy shouts at the kid closest to Tally. "It's called my fist in your face, if you don't get out of here right now!"

"Get lost!" orders Jasmine to the others.

Ayesha puts her arm around Tally's shoulders and leads her away, towards the safety of the wall.

"Are you OK?" asks Luke, jerking his head at Tally.

She nods, unable to risk opening her mouth in case sobs come out instead of words.

"Do you want us to do something about that lot?" Ameet cracks his knuckles and glares menacingly at the year seven kids who are slinking away, their faces red with embarrassment.

"Oh, well done," scoffs Ayesha, as she and Lucy join them. "Offer to sort them out when they're already gone. Very brave!"

"They're just stupid kids," says Lucy, seeing Tally's face. "Ignore them. They don't know what they're saying."

They do, though. Tally knows that. They've seen her stimming at school and they've been laughing about it behind her back. And now they're laughing about it in her actual face and, quite honestly, she isn't sure which is worse.

"They won't bother you any more," says Jasmine. "We told the loudest one that we'd wait for him outside the gates and beat him up if any of them even looked at you again."

Tally swallows hard. "Is everyone in school laughing about me being autistic?" she asks quietly. "I thought people kind of understood a bit more now."

Lucy shakes her head. "Don't worry about it," she assures Tally.

There's a ripping sound and then Luke holds out a big bag of chocolate buttons.

"I was saving these for later," he says. "But after all that drama I think we might need them now."

"How old are you?" mocks Lucy. "Those are for little kids."

"Feel free not to have any, then," says Luke sweetly. Lucy flashes him a grin and sticks her hand into the bag, emerging seconds later with a fistful of chocolate buttons. Luke proceeds to offer them around and Tally watches as hand after hand pushes into the bag, rummaging around in the contents.

"Thanks." Jasmine plunges her hand inside and Tally shudders. She's next, and there is no way that she can eat anything that's been handled by so many unwashed fingers. But Luke skips straight past her and empties the remaining buttons into his own hand before tipping them into his mouth.

It's *fine*.

She didn't want them anyway.

Now she doesn't have the awkwardness of refusing, and looking like she thinks she's better than the rest of them, when she quite clearly isn't better than anyone.

In fact, she's at the very bottom of the pile and she mustn't ever forget it.

"Here. This is for you."

Tally looks up to see Luke holding out a small bar of chocolate. She hesitates, unsure about what she's supposed to do and he gives her a quick nod.

"I know you don't like eating food that other people have touched," he tells Tally. "So I got you this when I bought the buttons."

Tally still doesn't move, so Luke pushes the wrapped bar into her hand.

"I don't know what to say," Tally whispers.

It's true. She's never had this experience before and

can't even begin to figure out what words are the right ones.

Luke shrugs his shoulders. "It's no big deal. I wasn't going to leave you out, was I?"

He turns to Ayesha and shoves the empty chocolate bag towards her. "You get to put this in the bin," he says. "As payment for eating my chocolate."

Ayesha instantly starts complaining about the fact that *everyone* ate it and why should it be her who has to walk *all the way* across the yard to the bin and couldn't he just put it in his bag, and then Lucy tells her to stop being such a moaner and Ameet joins in and Tally zones out, her head full of what Luke just said.

He wasn't going to leave Tally out.

Tally stares at the chocolate bar clutched in her hand. Luke is wrong. It *is* a big deal. It's the biggest deal of all because it's not just the words, although they're nice to hear. It's what Luke *did*. It's what they all did to back her up when the year seven kids were being unkind. Tally hears a lot of words every day and she knows how sneaky they can be but this *doing* – this actually doing something nice and kind and friendly – this is new.

A warm feeling spreads up through her body, starting in her toes and travelling along her veins until every inch of her is wrapped in happiness. She might not have been entirely sure about hanging out with all of them before, but things have changed. She can see now that while they're a strong, intimidating force, it's kind of great to have that sort of backup on your side.

Being part of them can only be a good thing.

Right?

CHAPTER 16

Tally dreams. It is last year, and she's at GoCamp with Gory and Jade, hanging out with the cute animals at the animal sanctuary. She laughs at something funny Gory says and feels the warmth of Jade's arm slung around her shoulder, and everything is real and good and simple. And then she wakes up and the positive sensations vanish before she has even opened her eyes, only to be replaced by the *feeling*. Actually, it's more than a feeling; it's a churning, physical whirlpool in her stomach and it's impossible to ignore.

"Morning, sunshine!" trills Mum, entering the room. "It's a glorious day outside and it's nearly the weekend so there's lots to be happy about!"

Tally doesn't move. Happy is not an option for her today, even if it *is* Friday.

"Let's get you up." Mum flings back the curtains, not seeming to notice that the bright sunlight pierces straight into Tally's eyes.

"I can't."

Tally hears the words come out of her mouth and every muscle in her body tenses. She didn't mean to say it but it's the truth. She can't go to school – she knows that with every bit of herself.

Mum sits down on the bed. "Talk to me, honey. We've been through this over and over again and I need you to explain the problem to me." She leans over and gently strokes Tally's forehead. "I know it's tricky for you without Layla but what's going on in there, hey?"

If she weren't battling with the terrifying sensation of drowning inside her own body, Tally would almost want to laugh. Mum has asked that question as if it has a simple answer; like it's as easy as asking if Tally wants peanut butter on her toast. But the simple answer to her question is *everything* and there is nothing easy about that.

Everything is going on inside Tally's head and it feels like water under pressure, getting higher and higher and threatening to overflow the edges. She knows that she *should* be happy – she has some friends and really is a

152

part of the group, not just hanging on the edges – but it all still feels so risky. As if she's going to mess it up at any minute and lose everyone.

It's happened before with the friends she cares most about.

It's not the most illogical fear in the world.

Tally sits up and swings her legs past Mum, intent on getting out of the room as quickly as she can. She knows this feeling and it never ends well.

Mum sighs. "I've spoken to school again and they say that your grades are OK and you seem fine in class and you haven't even needed to use the Safe Space for a while." She looks down at Tally. "They think that you've made real progress since we had that last meeting with them. So why are you refusing to go in?"

The dam bursts. But instead of doing what it might normally do, and roar out into the room, it empties Tally of all ability to move or speak. As the pressure releases, it drains her of action and instead of sending her into an explosive rampage, her body takes control in a new way.

There is no screaming because there is no air in her lungs.

There is no throwing or breaking because there is no strength in her arms.

There is no running because there is no power in her legs.

All that remains is emptiness.

And it is the worst feeling Tally has ever experienced.

Mum is speaking, but Tally can't understand what she's saying because some of the words seem to be missing. Somehow, she's got herself wedged into the gap between the wardrobe and the end of her bed and all she knows for sure is that she cannot leave this place. She curls into a small ball and puts her hands over her head. When she's having a meltdown she often makes a lot of noise and, sometimes, when she can feel a meltdown approaching, she'll sing one of her favourite songs to keep herself calm. But this isn't a meltdown. It isn't red and hot and volcanic. She doesn't know what's happening, but it's the opposite of those things. This is blue. This is cold. This is a blizzard. And she is stuck in it, with no idea about how to get out.

It lasts for ever, like an ice age.

At one point, Tally vaguely registers Mum leaving the room and then she's back, her mobile pressed against her ear. She crouches down in front of Tally and speaks urgently into the phone. Occasional words and phrases push themselves through the fog and into Tally's ears but they make no sense.

Silent.

Detached.

Won't respond.

Tally has no idea how long she's been there, in her safe little cave away from the snow and wind and ice. She knows that she feels bad, because her head is writhing in pain, but she doesn't know what *bad* might mean. Is she angry? Does she feel guilty? Is she unwell or scared or hurt?

Time passes, and slowly, so very slowly, other sensations start to creep in. It was impossible to even think about moving when her legs weren't properly connected to the rest of her body but now she can feel a tingling in her toes and a cramp in her left thigh from where she's been curled up. And sounds are trickling in too.

"Are you OK?"

Mum's voice is quiet but filled with fear. Tally wants to reassure her; tell her that she's fine but her throat feels tight and her mouth is dry.

Plus, it would be a massive lie.

The effort of moving is almost too much. It's as if

someone has wrapped her in a weighted blanket and her entire body feels laden down. But her legs are aching and her hands are cold and she can't stay trapped in between the wardrobe and the bed for ever. She's going to have to get up.

Struggling against the heaviness, Tally sits up and leans her back against the wall.

"There you are," says Mum, relief chasing away the fear. "You're back!"

I never went away, Tally wants to tell her. *I was always here*.

But it's too difficult to speak.

Tally sits in the living room, curled up on the sofa watching *Peppa Pig*. Peppa's little brother George does something silly and she smiles a little, just as Mum sticks her head around the door.

"Are you feeling a bit better?" she asks, handing Tally a plate of sandwiches.

Tally pauses for a second and thinks about it. She isn't entirely sure what Mum means by *better* but the scared, bad feeling has been replaced by a numb, slightly blurry sensation that makes her feel like all her energy has been drained away like bathwater going down the plughole. It doesn't feel good but it *is* definitely better than whatever it was that happened to her in the bedroom.

"A bit," she croaks, her throat strangely scratchy. "Although I'm still too tired to go to school."

"We should talk about that," says Dad. He rushed back in through the front door not long after Tally moved from the floor to the sofa, and he's stayed close by for the last few hours. Now he sits next to Tally and turns off the television. Mum sits on her other side and Tally tenses. She's telling the truth about being too tired for school and she hasn't got any fight in her today.

"I've spoken to the autism support worker and also to your school," starts Mum. "And we've all agreed that you feeling this way isn't acceptable."

"I can't help it," Tally says, staring at her plate. "I'm not choosing to do all of this, you know?"

"We *do* know," Dad tells her. He turns to look at Mum. "What was it you said the support worker called it, again?"

"Anxiety based school avoidance," says Mum. "It's not school refusal if Tally doesn't feel that she has a choice." She puts her hand on Tally's knee. "And I didn't mean that *you* aren't acceptable – I meant that it's not OK for you to feel this way about having to go to school."

Tally's head whips up and she stares at Mum. "Are you saying that I don't ever have to go back?" she asks, barely able to believe it.

"Not quite," says Dad.

Tally sinks back against the cushions and takes a tiny bite of a sandwich, although it's completely tasteless. She should have known better than to think they'd actually understand. Mum has got it right about the school anxiety but how does just *knowing* that make any difference, if they're still going to make her go?

"We've come up with a plan." Mum puts her hand on Tally's knee. "These tricky days are happening a lot and so school has agreed with us that we need to make a couple of changes."

"Like what?" asks Tally suspiciously. Change is not her favourite thing and she doesn't really see how adding even more stress to her week is going to help.

"We've spoken before about taking you out of all your PE lessons," Dad tells her. "But then you'll be missing out on getting any exercise. And the school thought you could stay out of lessons like French and music and drama and go to the inclusion unit instead for some work in a smaller group – but those are subjects that you really enjoy, aren't they? It seems a shame to miss out on those."

Tally nods. There are other kids in her year who get removed from those lessons and have to do extra English and maths instead and she's always thought that they must be having an even worse time at school than she is, which is *really* saying something.

"So the new plan is that you can have one day a week where you don't go into school and, instead, you'll do something different," says Mum. "Something that will give you a bit of space to relax, get some fresh air and time to be active but also recharge your batteries."

"What *kind* of thing?" asks Tally, her face wrinkling. Being active isn't her favourite thing, and if she's allowed to have a day off school then she'd much rather spend it in her room, either sleeping or playing games on her iPad or maybe writing and playing a new song. *Those* are the things that help her relax – not fresh air and being outside.

"Well." Dad wiggles his eyebrows at her, as if he's excited. "We wondered if you might like to go and help out at Ginny's stables?"

Tally is on her feet in seconds, her plate tumbling to the floor, the rest of the sandwich forgotten.

"Yes!" she shouts. "I would love that!"

She throws Mum a high five and then Dad stands up

and pulls her in for a huge, long hug that lasts just a little bit too long and smushes her face against his scratchy, woolly jumper but she doesn't say a word because she knows that this is his way of telling her that he loves her.

When he finally lets her go, she steps back and beams at her parents.

"What day will I go?" she asks.

"That's the good part," Mum says, her face pleased. "We'll have a code word and you can tell me in the morning if you don't feel that you can go to school. You don't need to explain or justify it – the code word will let me know that it's a stables day and not a school day."

"But you only get one day a week," warns Dad, wagging his finger in a joky way. "So you're going to have to make some good decisions about when to use your code word."

Tally frowns. That sounds an awful lot like they actually *do* think she has a choice about whether she can go to school or not. What happens if she uses her code word on Monday and then wakes up on Wednesday with *the feeling*? And what if what happened today happens again? She couldn't even get off the floor, never mind all the way to school.

Mum interrupts her thoughts. "Ginny has one

particular horse that she wants you to help out with. And she doesn't mind when you go – we can just let her know that morning that we're coming."

Tally's mind floods with memories of Ginny's stables. She hasn't been back there since she was in year six, despite asking Mum and Dad all the time if she could. Riding lessons *cost the earth*, according to them, which always makes Tally cross because horse riding is one of the things she could be doing that literally *wouldn't* kill the planet, unlike both of them driving off to work in their gas-guzzling cars every day.

"Can we go there now?" she asks. "I can be ready in five minutes. Please?"

Mum shakes her head. "It's too late to go today," she says. "And, besides, I think you need to have a few quiet hours here, just while you recover from your shutdown."

So *that's* what it was. It's a good word for what happened to her, Tally agrees with that. She felt just like a computer with too many tabs open – eventually it all got too much and it just stopped working altogether. Maybe she just needs switching off and on again sometimes?

And Mum has a good point. While the thought of spending time with the horses gave her some energy, she really is tired. It feels a bit like she's done a long, underwater swim and now that she's come up for air, she needs some time to let her lungs and her head and her eyes adjust to the real world again.

It's all going to be fine, she reminds herself, as Mum and Dad leave her to chill out with Peppa. She's got friends and she's in the group and now she has something else good; something really positive to focus on. If it's a good day then she can go to school and hang out with Lucy and the others and surely the more time she spends with them, the more she'll understand who it is that they expect her to be. And maybe she won't miss Gory, Jade and Layla quite so much.

Plus, if she can't go to school then she can visit Ginny and the stables and spend time with animals who aren't going to ask anything of her that she can't give.

It's all going to be perfect.

Today's In-Depth Report:
School Anxiety Part 2
What Makes School so Hard?

The social

Sometimes being with friends is the one thing that makes me feel OK about going to school. But trying to maintain friendships on a daily basis is exhausting and if it's not gone well then I really struggle to make myself go in and face the music.

The learning

Lessons in my secondary school are one hour and thirty minutes each, which is way too long. They also move too fast for me to keep up, are too hard and usually involve too much listening to someone else talk for ages about something that it's really hard to get interested in.

The teachers

Even though the teachers are nice, having to be known and understood by so many different teachers is really hard. At primary, I just had to explain myself once, to my class teacher, and that was it. Now I have about twenty different teachers and every year I have to start again with a load of new ones. Also, not only do they have to get to know and understand me, but I have to get to know and understand them. Like, which teachers will let you make jokes with them, which ones won't? Which ones will insist you look them in the eye, which ones won't? Which ones will make you stand up in front of everyone if you get something wrong, which ones won't?

The discipline

Trying to remember all the rules is a nightmare. There are so many, like no talking in the corridors, don't take off your blazer, etc, etc, etc. And some teachers enforce some rules more than others. When you are focusing so hard on whichever rules you need to follow to stop you getting into trouble, it's hard to be able to focus on learning too.

The sensory

The terrible noise as soon as I arrive - the sound of so many kids talking, shrieking, arguing, laughing. I can't hear myself think, which always panics me. The smells - sweat mixed with overpowering bodyspray. School dinners, the polish from the floor, cheese and onion crisps, trainers. Ugh. The brightness of the horrible fluorescent strip lights and the walls all covered with brightly coloured words reminding us what we mustn't forget. The discomfort and demand of having to change from my clothes into my PE kit and back again, then the horror of being picked for teams and play games in a noisy, echoey, screechy, squeaky PE hall. No wonder my head hurts at the end of the day. I'm overstimulated, overwhelmed and overexhausted.

At school, I have to just grin and bear all of this, because if I don't then I get into trouble. And getting into trouble, or standing out for not joining in, would be even worse than all of the awful sensations.

Home is like being alone in your own pack of lions. You don't always get along with them, but you know you belong with them

At school, it's like being thrown in with the whole zoo.

CHAPTER 17

Waking up on the following Monday morning is different. Like always, Tally lies very still and waits while her brain and body adjust to the new day but, unlike every other day, she doesn't feel as anxious. If the *feeling* is there, then she can just text Mum the code word. It feels like the pressure is off now that she knows there's a Plan B.

She stretches her legs, opens her eyes and smiles. The *feeling* is nowhere to be found. It's a school day and she knows that she's got this. Everything is going to be fine.

And it's not just waking up that's different today. Tally walks down the corridor at break-time, trying to figure out what has changed. It's definitely true that school is a very different place when you've got people. Nobody has pushed in front of her to get into class and she's not been left to sit on her own when the teacher tells everyone to get into groups and those things are great, but there's something more. Something she can't quite put her finger on. And then it hits her.

Nobody is pointing at her as she walks past the lockers.

There is no sniggering or muttered whispers behind hands.

She hadn't realized how much those things had become the soundtrack of her school day until they stopped.

In fact, now nobody really seems to want to look at her *at all*. Probably because they're terrified that Lucy will have a go at them for "looking at her wrong" which is something that Tally has heard her screech on several occasions. The relief of not having to navigate her way through the negative attention is almost overwhelming.

"Tally!" Lucy beckons her over to where they're all gathered. "Where were you on Friday?"

Tally opens her mouth but Ayesha is already talking before she can formulate a reply. "This is excellent! I can't wait for lunchtime!"

The girls are huddled together but as Tally approaches

they move apart, creating a gap for her. She smiles, feeling happy.

"Look!" Lucy unfolds a piece of paper and shows it to Tally. "How brilliant is this?!"

Tally reads the note that is written in Lucy's neat handwriting.

To Millie,

Meet us on the stage at 12:30 if you want to hang out.

From Us

Tally nods. "That's nice," she says. "I don't think Millie really has any friends so she should totally join us."

There's a moment of silence and then Lucy bursts out laughing.

"You're so funny!" she tells Tally, clasping her arm tightly. "This is why we like you – you're hilarious!"

"Comedy gold!" snorts Jasmine. "As if we'd actually want to hang around with a loser like Millie!"

"As *if*!" splutters Ayesha. "God – can you *imagine*?"

They all look at Tally who stares back for a long, silent moment.

She thought that Millie seemed OK.

She thought that she was a little shy and quiet, but she's never caused Tally any harm.

She thought that as they'd taken in Tally, that maybe, just maybe, this could be a group where other kids could also find some sanctuary.

She'd thought wrong. And that's a shame, but she's not sacrificing her own safe place over a girl she barely knows. It's a zoo out there and she's not prepared to be fed to the hyenas. Better to be stuck inside the group than abandoned on the outskirts – especially as it's now one whole week since Layla flew off to America and she still hasn't texted Tally, even once.

"As *if*!" she sniggers, copying Ayesha and feeling a bit sick. "So what's going to happen if she turns up on the stage at twelve thirty?"

Lucy grins, serpent-like.

"Oh, she'll turn up," she assures Tally. "And that's when the fun and games will begin!"

Then she turns away and pushes the note through the slatted door of Millie's locker and Tally couldn't do anything to stop this now, even if she wanted to.

The rest of the morning passes quickly, as it always does, with facts about World War Two in history bleeding into techniques on shading in art, and by the time the bell rings for lunch, Tally's head is spinning. She often thinks it would be so much easier if she could have a whole morning on one subject, just to give her brain time to process all the information and find ways to store it so that she can easily find it again. The constant rushing from one topic to another makes it impossible to put things into their own boxes, and by the end of each day she has one big, crammed box in her head labelled "school" that's overflowing with numbers and words and concepts and worries.

It's not an ideal way to learn anything, she knows *that* for sure.

The girls are waiting for her in the corridor outside the lunch hall. As they're about to enter, Tally sees Annie walking towards them, her unicorn hair flowing in long, colourful waves down her back. Lucy spots her too and raises her hand, beckoning her to join them, which is strange, because since that day at the shopping centre she's only said horrible things about the other girl. It looks for a second as if Annie is going to stroll straight past but then she changes her mind and walks with them across the hall to their usual table, right at the front next to the stage.

"How's it going?" she asks Tally. "I haven't had a chance to talk to you for a while."

Tally's face reddens. Annie is in her maths class but ever since the disastrous shopping day the other week she's been avoiding her. It just seems like the wisest choice. Annie is risky and Tally knows that hanging out with her could threaten everything she's worked to achieve with Lucy and the others. Plus, she knows what Tally *did* and that makes her difficult to look at.

"I've been around," she mutters. "It's been busy, that's all."

Annie glances at the rest of the group. They are laughing and looking around the hall and there is obvious expectation in the air.

"What's going on?" she asks Tally quietly.

Tally pulls out her lunchbox and doesn't answer.

"The lunchtime entertainment," says Lucy, leaning across the table, "is about to start!"

Annie frowns but before she can talk there's a crashing sound and Millie stumbles on to the stage.

"Oh my god!" snorts Ayesha. "Could she maybe draw a little more attention to herself?"

Lucy swivels in her seat to get a better view of the stage. "And now we *place our bets*," she tells the rest of them. "How long do you think she's going to wait up there for these new-found *friends* to turn up?"

"One minute!" Jasmine smirks.

"No *way*," calls Ayesha. "She'll stay for thirty seconds and then leg it!"

They're both wrong, Tally knows that. Kids like Millie might be terrified of getting the wrong kind of attention, but they'll put up with a lot if there's a chance it will get them some friends.

She should know.

"Five minutes," she says absent-mindedly. The rest of them whoop and cheer.

"That's brutal," purrs Lucy, gazing at her with what looks like admiration. "Even I wouldn't make her wait up there for that long."

"No – I didn't mean…" starts Tally, but it's too late. The damage is done. Ayesha is nodding enthusiastically, Jasmine is giggling so hard she can't even speak and everyone is shouting over each other and grabbing their phones to start their timers.

And Millie is still just standing there, in front of the whole of year eight, all alone.

Annie frowns. "This is cruel," she announces. "What are you lot even getting out of this?"

Lucy tilts her head to one side and gives Annie an innocent look. "It's *just* a joke," she tells her. "We're not hurting her, are we?"

And this is exactly what Tally means about the truth being complicated. It's true that nobody is hitting or kicking or physically attacking Millie but that doesn't mean she isn't being hurt.

Damage doesn't have to be visible to be real.

"You need to place your own bet if you're sitting with us," Lucy informs Annie. It's a test – another chance for her to join the group and even though she knows it's so, so wrong, Tally crosses her fingers tightly and hopes that Annie will just go along with it.

Next to Tally, Annie grabs her lunchbox and stands up.

"You can't just leave her up there," she says. "It's not OK."

Tally looks up as Annie shakes her head in disgust and then walks off in the direction of the door that leads to the back of the stage. Luke and Ameet have just arrived and are standing a few paces away, watching the whole scene unfold. Ameet starts to move towards their table but Luke pulls him back, instead moving across to the other side of the canteen, as far away from both the girls and the stage as possible.

Tally watches them go and then turns back to the stage.

"It's been one and a half minutes!" announces Lucy. "The girl has got stamina, I'll give her that!"

"What's *she* doing?" yells someone else and now other people are turning towards the stage, noticing the quiet girl with shaking legs, standing all alone.

"Are you going to sing us a song?" shouts someone else. "Get on with it!"

The hall rings with derisive laughter and Tally feels her stomach starting to churn.

"Just walk away," she mutters under her breath. "Let it go."

But Millie can't hear her, and even if she could Tally knows that she wouldn't listen; not while there's a chance of finally being part of a group at stake.

"Two minutes!" calls Jasmine. "Come on, Millie – you can do this!"

"Absolutely!" Lucy raises her voice to be heard above the whistles and shrieks coming from the other tables. "I'm sure your new *friends* will be arriving any time now! Loser!"

The girl on the stage hears and her eyes flicker across to their table, her confusion clear.

"What on earth is going on?" Mr Kennedy storms through the hall, his face screwed up in rage. "Be quiet, the lot of you – unless you want an entire year group detention."

The hall falls silent.

And then he notices Millie.

"You!" he hollers, pointing his finger. "I have no idea what you think you're doing but get down from there *right now*."

Millie's eyes well up and Tally can tell it's taking every ounce of strength that she possesses not to burst into tears.

"The stage is off limits at lunchtime, as you very well know," bellows Mr Kennedy, clearly in a worse mood than usual. "I'll see you in my office in exactly two minutes and you can expect to be in detention for the next week, young lady." He glares at Millie and then turns to look at the lunchtime supervisors. "Please can you keep *some* degree of control in here?" he spits, and then he spins on his heel and stomps back out of the hall.

The room is silent until he turns the corner, but

then the clapping starts. First one and then another, until the entire canteen is on their feet, giving Millie a standing ovation. All except Tally, who stays in her seat, her heart beating in tempo to the applause. Millie's red, humiliated face crumples and then there's another sound of crashing as Annie pushes through the costume and props boxes that are haphazardly stacked in the wings and runs out on to the stage, grabbing Millie by the hand and leading her away to safety, to somewhere she can cry without being watched.

"That was brilliant!" gasps Ayesha, once everyone has settled back down. "Honestly, Lucy – totally classic!"

"It was unkind," murmurs Tally. "You shouldn't have done it."

Lucy turns in her direction, her face surprised. "What do you mean?" she asks. "You were part of putting the note in her locker and it was *you* who suggested leaving her up there for five minutes, Tally. I was just going to let her stand there for a few seconds and then explain it was a joke – it was *you* who pushed it too far."

"No, I didn't mean it like that," Tally stutters.

Lucy looks at her sympathetically. "It's OK," she tells her. "Nobody's going to snitch on you – we've already proved that. Are we?"

The others shake their heads.

"Of course not," agrees Ayesha. "It was amazing! Harsh, but amazing."

"I didn't know you could be so savage, Tally," adds Jasmine. "Remind me not to get on the wrong side of you!"

They all laugh and then Lucy starts talking about her latest YouTube success and Tally is left alone with her thoughts.

After this, she is pretty sure that she *only* has a wrong side. Because there is nothing right about what just happened, but she has no idea about what she can do to make it better. Not if she wants to avoid standing in Millie's shoes.

CHAPTER 18

Cat Appreciation Group Chat

Jade: hey you guys

Gory: hey Jade

Jade: are you there, tally?

Tally: ...

Gory: hey tally! how's it all going?

Jade: just let us know how you're doing, ok?

Gory: ok?

Tally: ...

Gory: we know you're there. we can see you.

Jade: I don't think she wants to talk today, gory. that's ok, isn't it? we're right here when you need to chat, tally.

Gory: sure. except what if we want to talk about our stuff? Friends are supposed to listen to each other.

Jade: exactly. so we'll listen to each other and we'll listen to tally when she's ready to talk.

Gory: this is stupid. do you even want to be friends with us any more, tally?

Tally: ...

Gory: just answer us! we can see the dots – we know you keep typing a message.

Jade: leave it, gory. she's gone.

CHAPTER 19

She knows it's a bad day the moment she opens her eyes. The *feeling* is churning around inside her head and there is no way that she can go to school, not today. Reaching for her phone, Tally texts one word to Mum.

Stables.

She sinks back on to her pillow and waits for the bad feeling to disappear, but nothing happens. She thought she'd feel relief about not going in, but if anything she feels even *more* anxious now that she's used the code word. She's going to miss so much stuff if she isn't in school today. And what if she wakes up tomorrow and she feels even worse? Mum and Dad have made it very clear that the school have only agreed to one day off a week and that this is just a temporary solution.

The worry lasts through getting dressed and eating breakfast, and Tally starts to wonder if, maybe, just maybe, she'd be better off just going to school. But when she thinks about putting on her uniform and walking into the classroom, her head feels dizzy and her mouth goes dry and she knows that there's no way she can do it.

The drive to the stables simultaneously takes for ever and not long enough, and by the time they pull in through the farm gates any excitement that Tally might have felt is long gone. This is it. Her one shot at having something good. Her chance to do the thing she loves most in the world.

She is absolutely going to get it wrong and then riding will be spoiled for her, just like everything else.

Ginny is waiting for them when Mum stops the car. Mum gestures to Tally to remove her headphones and then gives her a big smile.

"Here we are, then!" she says. "You're going to have such a good day!"

Tally doesn't move. Mum shoots her a quick look and then gets out to greet Ginny. Tally can see Mum gesturing towards the car and she lowers her gaze. She's changed her mind. Coming here was a terrible idea.

She's only going to mess it up, just like she messes up everything. And then there will be nothing good left.

"Come on!" Mum has opened her door. "Ginny has got lots of wonderful things planned for you today."

"I want to go home," Tally mutters. "Just get back in the car."

Mum sighs loudly, making Tally's head snap up in panic.

"You chose to come here," Mum tells her, voice fake-bright. "Remember? It was school or the stables. Come on, Tally – this is *supposed* to be something different. Out you get, you'll be fine once you get started!"

There is the sound of someone clearing their throat and Ginny appears next to Mum.

"One of my horses is called Nigel," she says, and it isn't clear whether she's speaking to Mum, Tally or herself. "And sometimes he gets spooked by something and just freezes where he is. Some people would tell him off or use the whip to make him keep walking, but I don't allow that kind of behaviour here. I know that the best way to help Nigel face his fears is to dismount and gently lead him past whatever it is that is scaring him, rather than forcing him to confront it by himself."

She clears her throat again and looks directly at Mum. "Why don't you go and make yourself a cup of tea? There's a kettle in the tack room and you should be able to find some milk somewhere."

"Oh." Mum looks a bit startled. "Right, then. Yes, of course." She looks down at Tally. "You know that you can't just sit in the car all morning, don't you?"

"There are teabags next to the kettle," Ginny states bluntly. "Goodbye."

Mum frowns but she follows Ginny's instructions and heads off towards the barn. Ginny instantly turns away, leaving Tally's car door wide open, and strides in the direction of the teaching arena. Tally watches as Ginny climbs over the fence and then jumps down on to the sandy ground. Her feet have barely hit the floor when a horse trots across from the far side, his nose pushing repeatedly against her pocket. Ginny's laugh floats back on the warm breeze, bringing with it the scent of hay and manure and the dry horse smell that Tally loves so much.

Slowly, she swings her legs out of the car and stands up. She'll just watch from a distance.

In the arena, Ginny strokes the horse and mutters quietly into his ears.

Tally take a step forward, first one then another. Maybe getting a little closer will be OK.

Ginny rubs the horse's nose and he gives a snickering sound that makes Tally's heart pound faster. She walks to the fence and folds her arms across her chest. She'll stand here to make Mum happy and she won't have to go to school today. Nothing can go wrong if she doesn't go near the horse and she won't spoil anything which is *definitely* what will happen if she gets too close. Because horses know. They can tell what kind of a person you are and if you're the wrong kind of person, they won't want anything to do with you. And Tally knows that if *that* happened, she would never, ever get over it.

So she stands by the fence and watches while Ginny talks to the horse and rubs him down with her hands, and everything is starting to feel like it might be OK.

But then the horse messes it all up by noticing Tally.

There's no time to react. He's over by the fence in seconds and the smell of him fills her nostrils. He sniffs and Tally stiffens, knowing that he's determining who she is. And then his long face pushes against hers and he whinnies softly and even though it can't possibly be true, Tally feels for a brief moment like he's telling her it's all going to be fine.

"This is Nigel," says Ginny. "He likes you."

Tally takes a step back.

"He's an old boy now," continues Ginny, ignoring Tally's slow retreat. "Most of the kids that come here don't want to ride him because he doesn't always do as he's told. But he just needs to be with people who understand that being scared can look a lot like being difficult."

Tally pauses.

"Do you know what I sometimes do when I'm frightened?" Ginny taps her boot on the ground. "I get really, really grumpy and occasionally I shout at people and tell them to leave me alone, but it doesn't help. So I'm trying to remind myself that when I'm scared, maybe going deep inside myself doesn't actually make things any better."

Tally walks forward again and rests her hands on the fence. "I do that too," she confesses. "Especially the shouting."

"Us autistic folk can sometimes find it hard to explain how we're feeling," says Ginny, reaching across and taking a riding hat off the fence post. "Especially when we're scared. But if we can walk slowly and calmly past the fear then the rewards make it worth it."

Tally swallows hard. It feels strange to have a conversation like this with an adult – one where they actually say stuff that makes sense – but she remembers it being like this when she was here the last time. Ginny is the only autistic adult that Tally has ever met, and she can't help wondering if school would maybe be a bit easier if there were some autistic teachers who could understand how she feels, without it having to be such a big deal?

"What is Nigel scared of most?" she asks.

Ginny chuckles. "Everything," she tells Tally. "You name it – he's scared of it. The wind and the rain and a leaf fluttering down from a tree when he isn't expecting it. He's scared of the dark and cars and dogs and other horses, which means that he's quite lonely because his fear stops him from enjoying the company of the rest of the team."

"How can he be lonely if he doesn't want to hang out with them?" asks Tally.

Ginny looks at her thoughtfully. "I didn't say that he doesn't *want* to be with them," she says. "I said he's *afraid* of them. They aren't the same thing."

Tally nods and looks at Nigel. Maybe they have more in common than she thought.

"Perhaps you should get him to join in with them a bit more?" she suggests.

Ginny shakes her head. "Nigel isn't like the other horses – it never really works when I put them together. He isn't comfortable with them and they don't treat him particularly well because they can sense that he's different."

Nigel takes this as his cue to whinny, and Tally's heart thuds.

"That's so sad." She reaches out her hand and gives him a gentle stroke on the nose. "Poor boy."

"Not at all," Ginny informs her. "It's far better for Nigel to stay on his own and keep his identity than it is for him to be part of the group and lose all sense of who he is. True happiness has to come from being at home in your own body, not from changing your shape so that other people will be happy with who you are. Nigel is Nigel-shaped and that's OK. He just needs reminding of that now and again."

Tally's hands start to flap. She automatically pulls her arms in to her sides to stop them but then sees Ginny staring at her again, her eyes loud with an unspoken question.

If happiness has to come from being at home in her

own body, then maybe she should let her body do its own speaking. After all, her stimming is just another way of expressing how she's feeling and sometimes her stims are somehow louder than the words that come out of her mouth, even if not many people know how to hear them.

Tally relaxes and lets her hands tell Ginny how she feels about what she just said.

Ginny waits for a few moments and then gives her a smile, before handing her the riding hat.

"Put this on," she says. "And then come into the arena."

Tally's arms still. Talking is one thing and stroking Nigel is another, but she isn't ready to ride him yet, she knows that for sure.

"Tally." Ginny's voice is quiet. "Stop thinking and climb over the fence."

"I can't," whispers Tally, putting her feet on the first wooden rung. "I'm going to get it wrong."

"I won't let you get it wrong," promises Ginny, reaching out a hand and guiding Tally's legs down and on to the ground. "Now, if I remember rightly, you were a natural when you rode Peaches last time. Let's just pop you on to the saddle and you can sit up there for a bit."

Before Tally can formulate an argument, Ginny has given her a boost-up and she is astride the old horse, her legs dangling on either side of his flank. She's just sitting. Even she can't mess up *sitting*, surely?

"Now take hold of the reins." Ginny's voice is soft, almost like a lullaby and Tally does as she says. "I'm going to hold the lead rope and we're going to take Nigel here for a little stroll."

"No!" Tally's back tenses. "I can't do it! I want to get off!"

"Of course," Ginny assures her. "I'm not going to ask you to do anything that you don't want to, OK? But to get off safely we just need to walk him across to the corner. Do you think you can do that, Tally?"

Tally pauses, her legs jiggling up and down in the stirrups as she lets her brain contemplate the question. Ginny waits quietly and there is no rush, no demand to give any answer except the one that feels right to her. Tally takes a deep breath and nods at Ginny.

"I can try," she says, because that's all she can ever do and because she knows that is all Ginny will ever ask of her.

And then they're walking, and she can feel Nigel's steady movements beneath her, his body rippling as he plods his way across the sandy ground. Her hands clutch tightly to the reins and she leans forward slightly, scared she's going to fall off, but then Nigel tosses his head and gives a little sigh and it hits her. The connection between her and the horse replaces everything else.

How could she have forgotten this?

This is when she is happy. *This* is when she feels good in her own body.

How could she have doubted that this is the one thing she can do right?

"OK," declares Ginny. "It's safe for you to get off now. Shall I help you get down?"

Tally looks up and sees that they have reached the corner. "No," she breathes. "Please. Can we take him for a longer walk?"

Ginny looks up at her. "We can," she says. "But then we're going to have some jobs to do. We're going to need to untack him, and groom him properly. And after that there's the stable to muck out and the tack to clean."

"I don't mind doing all of that," Tally tells her. "I promise."

Ginny nods. "Very well, then. We need to be back by eleven o'clock because I have another lesson to teach, but I'll set you up in the tack room and you can work alongside Saira. She'll show you what to do." She glances at her watch. "It's ten fifteen now, so we have plenty of time."

Tally smiles. Ten fifteen on a Tuesday means maths. Right now, she could be squished behind a desk in an airless room with horrible fluorescent lighting that hurts her eyes, struggling to understand anything that's being said. She'd already be crumpled and fake and all out of shape, and by lunchtime she'd have nothing left to give. But instead, out here with Ginny and Nigel and the whole sky above her, she feels real and free.

She's Tally-shaped for the first time in a long time.

I feel most Tally-shaped when

- Other people aren't judging me.
- I'm riding a horse, feeling all my problems disintegrate with each stride.
- I'm in a safe spot, like tucked under my covers in bed with Peppa Pig.
- It's a Saturday morning and I suddenly remember I don't have school and that heavy feeling in my soul turns into joy.

Five reasons why horses are the best animals ever

1. They are definitely the most elegant, mysterious and beautiful creatures.
2. Their calm energy radiates on to me.
3. When I'm with them, I forget all my worries and feel accepted and not judged.
4. I can ride them, unlike most animals. This is a huge bonus.
5. When I'm on a horse, the way it moves and the way I move with it is really rhythmic and soothing.

CHAPTER 20

"Where were you yesterday?" Lucy's hands are on her hips and she is staring at Tally with distrust in her eyes. "We missed you."

Tally doesn't know why, but she suddenly feels nervous. Spending the day at the stables with Ginny and Nigel was wonderful but as soon as she got home, the worries started to invade and she hardly slept last night. Not that Mum and Dad helped with that – when she tiptoed across the landing to their room all she could hear was their muttered conversation coming from the other side of the door. Which at least was better than the not-muttered full-on argument about the electricity bill that erupted this morning while she was trying to eat her breakfast. All she could do was put on her headphones and drown them out with her favourite playlist.

"I had to go somewhere," she murmurs, not wanting to tell them the truth. Nigel and Ginny don't belong in the canteen of Kingswood Academy. Nobody here would understand them.

"You have to tell us if you're not going to be in," Lucy instructs her. "Anyway, more important is how many comments I got on that lip tutorial! Seriously – there were so many that I couldn't even read them all!" Lucy's eyes are shining as she looks around the group. "One person said I'm an *inspiration* – isn't that amazing?"

"Well, it's true," Ayesha tells her. "You're *totally* inspiring."

Lucy blows her a kiss and then pulls out her phone to show them the latest video that she's posted. Tally tries to make it look like she's watching, but inside her thoughts are whirring. She knows that Lucy is doing really well with her makeover channel but what she can't figure out is *how*.

How does she get so many people to watch her stuff?

How can she have so many subscribers when all she's talking about, day after day, is boring make-up?

And how does she make people *listen*?

"There's hardly anyone in school who isn't following you," says Jasmine, sounding a little envious. "It's like everyone wants to hear what you've got to say."

Tally nods. It's exactly like that and, even though she knows it makes no sense, she can't help feeling that the more people are listening to Lucy, the less people are able to hear a word that Tally says.

The bell rings and the girls pick up their bags, each heading off to different lessons. Tally checks her timetable and sees that she's got drama. Last year she was with Lucy and Ayesha but this year none of the girls are in her class. At least she's still taught by Mrs Jarman – nobody would ever think about giving her a hard time in front of the fierce but fair teacher.

Pushing open the door, Tally does what she always does and quickly checks the room. It's the same as always, with groups of kids hanging around the edges, ready for Mrs Jarman to appear and issue them with the warm-up task. She starts to move across to her usual lone spot by the desk and then pauses. Ginny said that she shouldn't have to change to make people like her and she knows that she's been squished and squashed so much that she's done things she would never had done if she'd been Tally-shaped. And so, even though the thought terrifies her, she knows what she has to do if she's going to try to be herself once more.

Changing direction, she heads across to the opposite corner where another girl is carefully placing her bag on the floor.

"Hey—" she starts, and then Mrs Jarman dashes through the door.

"Sorry I'm late!" she calls. "There was an emergency in the staffroom and I got delayed."

"Did someone steal Mr Kennedy's coffee cup again?" someone shouts.

Mrs Jarman spins round. "It was his chocolate biscuits, actually – and if you know anything about that, Olly Daniels, then you'd better speak up."

There's a moment of silence and then Mrs Jarman grins, causing a ripple of laughter to spread around the room. "OK, I'd like you to get into groups of four and then you've got five minutes to play a quick round of Unique and Shared. Find out what characteristics you have in common, as well as anything about you that might be unique. Off you go."

Everyone starts moving into groups. Luke and Ameet walk across to where Tally is standing and she gives them a brief nod, before turning to the girl beside her.

"You can be in our group, Millie," she says. "Who's going to start?"

Millie looks down at the floor and Tally frowns. She was trying to make up for what happened in the hall by including her instead of making her wait until everyone else was in a group, which is what usually happens.

It was supposed to be a nice thing – but it's not going to be enough.

"I'll go first," offers Ameet, sitting on the floor. The rest of them join him. "OK. Something that's unique about me are my incredible football skills."

"No way," objects Luke. "I'm just as good as you are, maybe even better!"

"So that's a shared characteristic," says Tally diplomatically. "OK – how about me? I'm autistic and that's pretty unique."

"Is it, though?" asks Luke, looking thoughtful. "I mean, I didn't know anyone else who was autistic when we were in primary school but there's quite a few people in our year now. So it's not *that* unique, is it?"

Tally scowls. "I think you will find," she informs him, "that no *one* autistic person is like another. So, yes – I am *absolutely* unique, thanks very much."

Luke puts his hands up. "Sorry! I didn't mean to offend you or anything! So, my thing is, I really like watching *Peppa Pig*. Does that make me unique?"

"It makes you a *loser*," scoffs Ameet, wincing when Luke smacks him on the arm.

"I like *Peppa Pig* too," admits Tally, before she can think about it. "It makes me laugh."

Luke nods. "Peppa is seriously underrated brilliance," he agrees. "You know that homework we had to do on *Animal Farm*? Well, I managed to include Peppa and her little brother George in my essay."

"What did miss say?" asks Tally, and even Millie raises her head, looking curious.

Luke shrugs. "She said that I had *failed to understand the task* and made me do it again," he tells them. "'S'not my fault that she doesn't appreciate the links between popular culture and the classics."

Ameet snorts and Tally turns to Millie.

"How about you? What's unique about you?"

Millie stares at her for a moment. "I don't know," she says calmly. "But why don't you tell me. You seem to think that you know who I am."

"I don't really know you." Tally takes a deep breath and stares at her shoes. "But OK. I think that you're kind because I saw you looking after one of the year sevens who fell over by the gates. I reckon you're pretty clever because you always have the answer in our science lessons even though you never put your hand up. I'm guessing that you like sunflowers because you've got loads of stuff with them on. And the one thing I *do* know for sure is that you really didn't deserve for us to put that note in your locker and leave you up on the stage in front of everyone."

Tally pauses and then looks up at Millie's face. "I'm really sorry," she says finally. "It was a horrible thing to do and I know that you probably hate me now. And I don't really like that idea but I can't change what I did. I'm sorry."

"Once the last person has had their turn, you can all gather in the middle of the room while I hand out the scripts," calls Mrs Jarman.

Luke and Ameet leap up immediately, leaving Tally alone with Millie.

"How do you know all that about me?" asks Millie, not moving.

Tally exhales slowly. "I notice stuff? I saw you and, if it makes any difference, I thought it'd be great if you were part of our group."

"You let me completely humiliate myself in front of the whole year." Millie shakes her head. "You have no idea how bad that made me feel."

"I do," confesses Tally, feeling her cheeks start to redden. "I know exactly what that feels like, which probably makes me even worse than the others, because at least they don't know what's it like to be on the outside. Nobody laughs at them, so they don't get it – but I do."

"I thought you were just like them," Millie tells her. "Part of their group."

Tally's hand start to flap.

"I didn't mean to make you sad," she says. "If I could take it back then I would – I promise. I wanted to fit in with the others but I never wanted to hurt you."

Millie looks at her for a long moment and then stands up.

"You can't take back what you did," she tells her. "But I guess we all do stuff we're not proud of. Maybe things can be a bit different from now on? If you really mean it?" She reaches one hand down and pulls Tally to her feet.

"I really mean it," Tally says, her heart thudding with relief and nerves and, maybe, just the tiniest feeling of hope.

Words can never completely remove the hurt that actions have caused. Tally knows that better than anyone else. But maybe they can help heal some of the wounds? Maybe words can form a bridge between her and Millie that will allow Tally to show the other girl who she really is. Perhaps words *do* matter, as long as what you're saying and what you're doing are the same thing.

CHAPTER 21

It's a stables day. Tally somehow managed to stagger through the final two days of school last week but all the masking and pretending means that she's spent almost the entire weekend either in bed or watching her programmes on the iPad and dreading the week ahead. Tally isn't sure that there is any feeling in the world as awful as the one she gets on a Sunday afternoon, when the clock starts to speed up and every minute is bringing her closer to Monday morning.

So it is definitely a stables day but despite the relief of not having to go to school, Tally still feels awful inside. She has her lesson with Ginny, who can tell that something isn't right and lets her ride around the paddock on Nigel without saying a word. Then Ginny takes her into the stables and tasks her with rubbing down the horse while she sorts out the tack nearby – close enough for Tally to feel safe but not so close that she can hear Tally's whispered conversation with Nigel.

"School is horrible," she tells him, brushing his body with firm strokes. "There's never any time to breathe properly, you know? It's not like out here, where you can take big, deep lungfuls of air and feel good about everything. I'm too busy running from one room to another and trying to remember what each teacher wants cos they're all different and they all run their classes in completely different ways. Like, Miss Perkins expects you to answer a question the instant that she asks it but Mrs Jarman doesn't mind if you take a moment to think about what you want to say. And Mr Simpson wants his class to be silent but Mrs Sheridan says that we have to talk or we're not learning."

She sighs and leans her head gently against his flank. "It's exhausting – and that's just the teachers."

Nigel pushes his nose into her hand and snorts.

Tally nods. "You're right. The teachers aren't the biggest problem. At least they know who they are. I don't think I even recognize myself any more."

She lowers her voice even further, only trusting Nigel with her next words. "I don't like me very much either, right now. But if I don't do what Lucy and the others want then I'm going to have nothing. Layla won't reply to my messages and being friends with the girls has *got* to be better than being a nobody, hasn't it?"

"I think that depends on how much it's costing you to be with those friends," says a voice, and for a wild moment Tally thinks that it's Nigel before realizing that a) horses can't speak and b) if Nigel *could* talk then he wouldn't have the voice of a middle-aged woman.

She spins round and sees Ginny leaning on the wooden wall of the stall.

"You were listening!" she accuses.

Ginny shakes her head. "I could hear you, but I wasn't listening," she says. "You might want to work on your quiet voice if you don't want to be heard."

Tally swallows. She *does* want to be heard. That's all she wants.

"I came over to tell you that your mum is here to collect you," says Ginny, opening the stall door. "I'll see you next week, OK?"

Tally gives Nigel one final pat on the nose and nods at Ginny.

"Remember what I said," the stable owner calls, as Tally reaches the main doors. "It sounds like being friends with these kids is coming at a bit of a cost – so just be sure that it's worth it. The best things in life should be free, that's what I've always thought."

Tally steps out into the sunlight. What Ginny is saying makes no sense. Everything comes at a cost, that's just the way it is. Ginny is great and she might understand what it's like to be an autistic girl but she's not in year eight, is she? She doesn't know what it's like to balance on a tightrope so thin that you could tumble off at any moment, the jeering of the crowd the last thing you hear before you hit the ground.

By teatime, Tally is exhausted and she only wants one thing: to be on her own, eat some pizza and go on her phone. She definitely doesn't want to sit around the kitchen table listening to Nell moan about how stressed she is while Mum and Dad have chirpy conversations about how lucky Tally was to go to the stables and how school tomorrow is going to be so wonderful and great.

"I need to eat in my room," she tells Mum.

"I thought we agreed we'd eat together as a family on school nights?" says Mum, as she puts the pizza on to a plate and hands it to Tally.

"It *has* been a long day," says Dad. "Maybe we should just try to get through one mealtime without any issues?"

"Well, if Tally isn't eating at the table, can I take mine upstairs too?" asks Nell. "Rosa is struggling with her history coursework and I said I'd help her."

Dad frowns. "Well, I *suppose* the same rule should apply to you too. Otherwise it isn't exactly fair…"

Tally rolls her eyes. Nell isn't going to talk to Rosa about history, she's quite sure of that. Unless it's the history between her and that boy she's constantly posting photos of on Instagram, his arm draped around her shoulders like a floppy old scarf. And Nell doesn't have the same challenges as Tally so she doesn't *need* to have the same rules. Fair should be about everyone getting what's right for them, not all having the exact same thing.

Once she's safely upstairs and inside her room, she can breathe properly. She's slipped Rupert up here too, which she's pretty sure Dad saw but pretended not to notice, and once he's snuggled up on her bed she turns on her fairy lights and the lamp that Nell bought for her birthday last year, the one with the pretend jellyfish floating around. Then she flops down next to him, grabs a slice of pizza with one hand and her phone with the other and starts to scroll through her messages. Gory and Jade have both tried to contact her several times since they fought in the group chat, but she hasn't replied. She misses them and their honest, funny conversations, but they're the only people she can actually be real with and the idea of telling them about how she's been behaving is truly awful. She's sure they'd never want to be friends with her ever again. Surely it's better not to talk to them than risk that?

Tally takes another bite of pizza and goes on Instagram, where she can see straight away that she has a message. Ignoring the fact that Nell has just posted a new photo, which means that she is absolutely *not* helping Rosa with her history coursework, Tally clicks on the message. It's from someone very unexpected and her heart starts to pound as she stares at Luke's profile picture.

The message is short.

Not sure if you've seen this or if I should even tell you but I'd want to know if it was me. Look at Lucy's latest post. Tally, they are NOT your friends.

With slightly shaking hands, Tally clicks on the link that Luke has sent her.

And there it is.

There *she* is.

She stares at her phone, trying to make sense of what she's seeing. She knows instantly when this was recorded – it's obviously from the day that she first met Annie, when someone dropped a tray in the canteen and it made a loud crashing sound that startled her. What she can't understand is how this video of her in the school canteen, humming and stimming and putting her hands over her ears can possibly be here, on Lucy's Instagram page. But then she remembers Lucy and Ayesha, huddled over Lucy's phone and giggling. They filmed her. They filmed her and now she's online. The clip itself is quite short but it's playing on a loop – an endless repeat of Tally, Tally, Tally.

And then she sees the comments and her already-churning stomach threatens to revolt. She scrolls down, seeing names and profile photos of people she knows. She sits next to these kids in maths. She walks beside them in the corridors. They breathe the same air as her and yet none of those shared experiences matter because alongside the pictures of their faces are their cutting, hurtful words.

Nut job.

Loser.

More laughing emojis than she can count, which are almost harder to handle than the words because being laughed at is the worst feeling in the world.

They aren't even trying to hide. *They* aren't ashamed of who they are.

Tally's fingers are trembling and it takes her several attempts to type out a private message to Lucy:

Please take down that video.

She can see that Lucy has received the message and navigates back to the offending post, wanting to see that it has gone with her own eyes. But nothing happens, other than yet more people are eagerly contributing their thoughts on Tally.

Why is she so weird?

Get a life already!

Tally swipes back and messages Lucy again and the next five minutes are a horrific cycle of messages sent into the wilderness, the only response being even more comments in the video.

Please, Lucy. I hate this. Take it down.

If I was like that then I'd never go out in public. She's crazy!

Why are you doing this? Stop it, now.

Why is she allowed to go to our school?
What's with the flapping?

I'm begging you, Lucy, just stop it.

God – I wish she'd just do the world a favour and disappear.

And now she can't type any more messages because she's crying so hard that she can't see her phone properly. All she can do is sit on the floor and watch it play out – watch the kids she has to spend hours of every day alongside assassinate her with words that scorch themselves so deeply into her mind she knows they'll never truly fade.

The comments finally stop after two relentless hours when Lucy posts a link to her latest YouTube video and everyone flocks to comment on that instead, but Tally doesn't move from the bedroom floor. She can't. She isn't sure that she'll ever be able to speak or move again. It's as if she only exists in the comments that everyone wrote, and all she can do is stay very still, watching the words dance in front of her, taunt her, silence her even further.

This is the worst thing that has ever happened to her and she has no clue what she's supposed to do now.

One thing about social media . . .

Social media helps me to connect with my friends and feel less isolated, but it can also have some real negatives. All that fakery can make girls feel uncomfortable in their own skin, and it's programmed to be addictive – the constant *ding* it uses makes you want to pick it up – so it's hard to stay away.

At first it seems like social media is this fun-loving and social world, but there are lots of things hidden behind the smiles and the people who look perfect.

Someone's life could be destroyed in one cruel minute – all it takes is a hateful comment or a mocking video that spreads like wildfire, and breaks someone into pieces in the process.

CHAPTER 22

It's not a school day or a stables day. It's a bad day.

A really bad day.

Nell walks into the living room and then ducks as the remote control whizzes past her head and hits the wall behind her, narrowly missing Dad's guitar.

"Leave me alone!" Tally screams, kicking out at the small coffee table and turning it on its side. "I hate all of you!"

Mum quickly launches forward to grab the mug that she'd placed on the table only seconds before, but it's too late. Hot coffee spills on to the new rug, making a massive splotch right in the centre. Tally watches as it seeps into the creamy-white wool.

"What's going on?" asks Nell. "And can it go on somewhere else? Rosa's coming over later and I want to lay out all my textiles work in here before I go to school."

"No, it cannot," hisses Tally, rounding on Nell. "There are other things happening in the world other than your stupid exams, you know."

"Mum?" Nell turns to look at her. "Please. Do something about her."

"Don't call me a 'her'!" Tally screams back, her face contorted with rage. "You know you're not allowed to say bad things to me."

"Let's give her a moment," says Mum, gesturing to Nell to leave.

"WHAT ABOUT ME?" bellows Tally. "You can't just leave me on my own."

"Make your mind up," mutters Nell. "You wanted to be left alone a minute ago."

"Nobody asked you!" Tally glares towards her sister, her eyes narrowed. "So just shut your mouth and go away."

Mum steers Nell across the room, turning to look at Tally as they reach the door.

"I'm not leaving you," she says, her voice low and slow. "But you need to calm down. Just stay here and have some peace and quiet for a minute, OK?"

Then they've gone and the door is closed quietly

behind them and Tally is left all alone.

No – that's not quite true. The feelings and sensations that are twisting and churning in her head make it feel like she's surrounded by chaos and noise and emotions. She'd do anything to feel the peace or the quiet that Mum suggested. It would be wonderful to be able to breathe, just for a second. Or to sleep. But it's all too much and her head can't even begin to figure out which noise is loudest which is why she's been awake all night.

Anger: Lucy betrayed her.

Anxiety: Nobody understands.

Disgust: She hurt Millie and she stole the top and those things were so, so wrong.

Confusion: Why is everything so hard? And how come the one person who tried to help her was Luke?

Fear: She's messed it all up, yet again. Her one shot at fitting in has disappeared.

Grief: Gory and Jade are gone, along with Layla. And she misses them so much it hurts.

Horror: Absolutely everything to do with school and Instagram and that video.

Tally flings herself on to the floor and stares at the mess of coffee on the rug. Even if Mum somehow manages to do something clever and remove the stain, it will still be there inside; dirty and horrid and ruined. And maybe everyone else will eventually forget about it and move on and when they walk into this room they'll just see a plain white rug. But not her.

She'll always know it's there.

"Tally?" Nell's feet come into view, followed by her face as she lies on the floor and stares at her sister. "What's wrong? Is it the girls at school again?"

Tally closes her eyes. Her head is still a tempest; a whirlwind of emotions that are so tangled together it's impossible to pull on one thread without disintegrating entirely. If she tells Nell about the girls then she'll have to talk about the shoplifting and Millie and losing her friends and the video – and she can't tell Nell about those things. Her big sister might be annoying and always moaning about her own life but the idea of her thinking badly of Tally is more than she can bear.

"I get it, you know." Nell's voice is quiet. "I've been there, Tally. School can be tough and kids can be cruel. But if you tell Mum and Dad about what's going on then they can help."

"Really?" Tally opens one eye and peers at Nell. "Are you honestly trying to tell me that when you had a problem at school you told Mum and Dad and the problem disappeared?"

Nell sighs. "Well – no. I guess not."

"Exactly." Tally sniffs loudly.

"But talking about it helped," Nell persists. "It made me feel a bit less on my own. Because you're *not* on your own, Tally. We've all got your back, you know?"

Tally nods. She *does* know that and it does help – sometimes. It's just that them all having her back doesn't solve the problems that are attacking from the front and the sides and above and below. What she needs is three hundred and sixty degree protection, and her family, no matter how much they try and how much they love her, are never going to be able to provide her with that.

CHAPTER 23

After the storm, comes the calm.

That's what's supposed to happen, anyway. Once Nell leaves for school, Mum comes back into the living room, bringing Tally's headphones with her. Tally lets Mum take her upstairs to her room and settle her down with her headphones and her phone, but the second Mum has gone back downstairs, she shoves her phone under her bed. There is nothing on there she wants to see or hear.

Then Tally lies back, her sparkly blue headphones over her ears, and lets the silence engulf her. And unlike the last time she shut down, this time isn't so bad. It feels less like being stuck in a cave and more like checking out from everything that's going on. It feels like the only thing she can do to keep herself safe.

At suppertime, she sits quietly, grateful for the first time that Nell always has so much to say. Mum casts her a few anxious glances but Tally eats her food and drinks her water and doesn't even kick off when Dad tells Mum that he's taken Rupert's bed out of the kitchen and put it in the utility room because it's starting to smell. It's like she's in the room but not quite – she knows that she's eating but she can't taste the food. She knows that Nell is talking but she can't hear the words. She knows that Rupert's bed shouldn't be in the utility room because it's cold and dark out there, but she also knows that she can't do anything about it. Everything feels very far away and as if it isn't really happening to her, and she wonders if this is how it feels to be a ghost.

At bedtime, Tally lets Mum tuck her under her duvet and turn on her nightlight and kiss her goodnight. She lies very still because she's incredibly tired, but her brain can't forget what happened in here last night and it also still can't seem to remember where sleep is found and so she gets up and wanders through the house. Up and down the stairs and in and out of the bathroom and finally into Mum's art studio where she stares at the large painted canvas on the wall and gets lost in the swirl of colours that Mum has titled *Frustration*. At some point Dad finds her and tries to encourage her back to bed but her body cannot rest and she's up again and back downstairs, this time to the kitchen where Mum makes her a warm drink that has no flavour and tells her that she has to sleep.

And then it's morning and she's still awake and her head is starting to hurt but it doesn't matter because her brain feels numb, so she doesn't really care. Her body is exhausted now and she sits slumped against the wall of the kitchen while Dad and Mum talk in hushed whispers on the other side of the room. If she could speak then she would tell them that they don't need to worry – she wouldn't be listening to them even if they were yelling.

"Let's snuggle you up on the sofa," says Mum, penetrating the fog. "You can watch some *Peppa Pig* and maybe have a little snooze."

Tally shakes her head.

"How about lying down in bed?" suggests Dad.

She doesn't bother responding. Her bedroom is tainted now too and when she's in there the only thing she can think about is the Instagram video. If she's going to find sleep it certainly won't be in there.

"Perhaps some fresh air will help?" wonders Mum,

and just to stop them from going on at her any longer, Tally nods and pulls herself wearily off the floor.

"Shall we go for a little walk?" asks Dad. "We could head to the shop and buy the newspaper?"

"I'm going in the garden," mutters Tally and then, before they can do anything unhelpful like trying to join her, she stumbles out of the back door and away down the path, past the old apple tree and towards the shed.

The roof of the shed was her favourite place to go last year. She would stand on the very top, feeling like she could soar and fly. When she was up there, she felt seen, she felt known, and it reminded her that she was bigger than any words that might be flung in her direction. She hasn't been up there for ages, though.

Slowly, carefully she makes her way up the ladder, avoiding the rotten third rung and clambering on to the roof. She's too tired to stand but she crawls upwards and swings one leg over the ridge, sitting astride the top and looking back towards the house where she can just see Dad peering anxiously through the kitchen window every few minutes, checking she's OK.

They are trying so hard to make things right for her but it's a constant battle because the things everyone says she has to do are the exact same things that are causing the problem. They've all come such a long way over the last few years and she knows that Mum, Dad and Nell can see her.

They know that there are lots of ways to be her and they know who she is.

But even *they* can't know what it's like to be constantly forced to shove all the pieces of you into a form that makes other people happy but feels so wrong for her. And all Tally wants is to be allowed to let her pieces settle into their natural shape.

So she sits and she breathes and she tries to make her mind empty of all thoughts, breathing in fresh new air and exhaling the awfulness of the last few weeks. And when her head is finally quiet, she slides back down the ladder and heads up the garden, before slipping quietly into the house and through to the utility room where Rupert is snoozing. She sinks down on the floor and when Mum comes searching, that's where she finds her. Curled up and finally asleep, on Rupert's old dog bed with the old dog cuddled beside her.

"I'm sorry I was late." Tally brushes Nigel's back with long, firm strokes. "I haven't been to school at all this week so Mum and Dad took ages to decide if it was

OK for me to still come here. It's like none of them are actually listening when I say I can't go in."

Nigel makes a harrumphing noise, which Tally takes as agreement.

"You're so lucky," she tells him. "You've got Ginny and she gets it. There's no way she's going to make you hang out with the other horses." She moves round to his other side. "She wouldn't let them be unkind to you either – and she definitely wouldn't tell you to *ignore* them and *let it go*."

She's being a tiny bit unfair here, she knows that. She hasn't actually told Mum or Dad or Nell about what happened with Lucy's post and the video and the comments, so she doesn't know for sure what they would say. They both spent ages last night trying to convince her to tell them what's going on and why she couldn't sleep – and she's been starting to wonder if maybe Nell was right and it might be better to talk to them. But it's a gamble because it will probably all come out wrong and they won't understand. And then she'll get upset and *upset Tally* often gets confused for *difficult Tally* and right now that's not a chance she's prepared to take.

"Do you want a lesson today?" Ginny is suddenly

there, leaning in her usual spot. "We've still got plenty of daylight left and Nigel could do with the exercise."

Tally hesitates and then shakes her head. The combination of a meltdown followed by a shutdown has left her feeling more drained than she's ever felt. When Mum agreed to drive her to the stables she was relieved, but she's actually too tired to ride today.

Ginny nods. "OK, well, in that case I think I'd better ask Saira to take him out." She glances at her watch. "Why don't you head home and I'll see you again in a few days? We could go for a longer ride – perhaps out into the fields?"

Tally frowns. "I can't come until next week now," she reminds Ginny. "They're going to make me go to school tomorrow."

Ginny smiles at her. "Next week will be here before you know it," she says. "Now hurry along to your mother and let me get Nigel set up for his ride."

Tally is quiet on the drive back and once they reach home she heads straight upstairs and retrieves her phone from under her bed, which is where it's been for the past three days. When she finally woke up in Rupert's bed she was still exhausted and there was no way she could have handled looking at it then. Yesterday was a bit better but she still didn't want to risk seeing something that would spiral her back into a bad place. She's not entirely convinced that she's ready now, but she can't ignore it for ever.

She plugs it in to the charger and then sits down on her bed, her fingers taking her through the various screens. She's got a message from Gory and another from Jade but she leaves them for later and instead swipes until she's looking at Lucy's account, scrolling to see what she's posted.

There's a picture of Lucy's cat and a selfie of her, Jasmine and Ayesha all blowing a kiss at the camera. There's a link to Lucy's latest YouTube tutorial and a photograph of an ice cream. But there is no video of Tally. It's like it's disappeared off the face of the earth, and her with it.

The notifications bar shows Tally that she has some messages and she opens them, desperately hoping the nasty comments on the post haven't somehow crawled their way into her DMs. But the messages are from Lucy and as Tally reads them, she feels something snap inside her.

Chill out.

It was just a laugh.

Stop stressing, Tally – you need to relax.

It's not a big deal. If you'd been in school all week then you'd know that.

Lucy isn't sorry. She doesn't feel bad for what she did.

She's laughing it off; pretending it was all a joke.

Tally reads them all once and then she reads them again. And then she thinks about what Ginny said to her the other week, about her friendship with the girls coming at a cost and being sure that it was worth it.

Well, it isn't. She can see that now. By trying to pay the price of belonging to the group, she's lost part of herself and it's not a fair exchange. And the one thing that Tally hates, more than anything else, is things being unfair. Different people need different things but it all has to be fair in the end.

Gory warned her. He asked her which was more important – being herself and speaking up or fitting in with the rest and staying silent.

When they made her feel awful about the make-up, she just let them get away with it.

When Millie was targeted with that awful note, Tally didn't intervene. She went along with it.

When they told her to steal the top, she didn't say a word. She did what they told her.

Tally has always thought that remaining loyal to her friends was the most important thing, but maybe that loyalty needs to go both ways.

Maybe it's time to open her mouth and say what she's really thinking. Because they might not want to understand how they've made her feel, but maybe it's time she tells them anyway.

I wish I could stand up for myself more. I can do it at home no problem, but that's because my family are my safe people, even though they probably trigger me as much as anyone. The thing is, I know whatever I do they will always be there. At school, it all feels too risky and I just can't build up the confidence. It feels even worse on the days when I've not had enough sleep, or woken up feeling bad.

I just wish I could reach inside myself and find my roar when I'm at school, but for some reason it stays hidden away deep inside me.

CHAPTER 24

"It was just for *laughs*!" Lucy smirks at Tally, flanked on either side by Jasmine and Ayesha. "Tell me that *isn't* why you've been off school for days? God – that's tragic!"

"Can't you take a *joke*?" enquires Ayesha.

"I like jokes," says Tally, trying to ignore the fact that her heart is threatening to leap out of her chest and thump away on the playground. "But jokes are supposed to be funny. And this *wasn't* funny."

Lucy shrugs and tosses her hair over her shoulder. "As you've already said, *several* times. But here's the thing. If we" – she gestures to the other two girls – "if *we* find it funny and you don't, then who is right? Why do *you* suddenly get to decide what's funny and what isn't?"

"Yeah, right," adds Jasmine. "What are you – the comedy police?"

"No." Tally shakes her head. "But it was a video of me, and people were saying horrible things about me, so I think I should be the one to say if it was funny or not."

Lucy sighs, as if the whole topic of conversation is incredibly boring. "Fine. You don't think it was funny. I've taken it down now, anyway, so you can stop banging on about it."

Tally swallows hard. This is where she's supposed to stop, she knows that. She's been allowed to have her say and the others don't agree with her and if she shuts up now, sure, she'll probably be punished by being ignored for the rest of the day, but she'll still be part of the group. She'll still have friends.

Except they aren't very *good* friends. And not-good friends are not really friends at all.

The thought somehow manages to creep in from the back of her brain, where it's been living for quite a long time, while simultaneously hitting her like a smack in the face.

These girls are not being good friends and they haven't been good friends for a really long time. It's like she has to keep on learning that the hard way.

Friends don't hurt you and then say that it's your fault.

Having friends shouldn't mean forgiving them for the same thing, over and over again.

Friends don't break you to fit you into their box. The best friends don't even *have* a box.

"You shouldn't have put it online in the first place," Tally tells Lucy. "It was cruel and unkind and you were only doing it to hurt me."

Lucy gasps and Ayesha springs forward.

"You can't talk to her like that!" she objects. "Apologize, right now!" She pulls Lucy into a big hug. "Just ignore her, Lucy. She's not worth it."

Tally's stomach flips, like it's filled with squirming snakes.

She's not worth it.

So, what *is* she worth, then?

"I didn't do it to hurt you," sniffles Lucy, dabbing at her eyes. "I can't believe you'd accuse me of such a horrible thing, Tally. Honestly – you've not even *been* here all week. You have no idea what's been going on."

"Yeah," adds Jasmine, scowling at Tally. "We've only ever tried to be nice to you and this is how you repay us? By accusing us of deliberately trying to make you sad?"

Beside her, Lucy bursts into sobs. "Why would I do that?" she pleads, gazing at Tally with eyes that are surprisingly dry. "It was just a bit of fun, that's all. Did I get it wrong? You're not going to tell on me, are you?"

"You totally didn't get anything wrong," Ayesha assures her. "It *was* funny. Anyone *else* would think it was funny, anyway."

"You've really upset Lucy," hisses Jasmine. "Well done. I hope you're happy now."

"No!" Tally's voice is louder than she intended. "I'm *not* happy! That's why I need to talk to you about this. Putting up that video for everyone to see made me feel really sad."

She's worth enough to say how she feels.

"Oh, *you* felt sad?" snarls Ayesha, patting Lucy on the back. "It's all about *you*, isn't it? What about poor Lucy? She's the one crying in the middle of school, not you."

"I didn't want to make anyone feel bad," starts Tally. "I just wanted to explain that—"

"Nobody wants to hear it," interrupts Jasmine. She turns her back on Tally and joins Ayesha and Lucy in a group hug. Tally stands there awkwardly. This is not going the way she hoped. She thought that she'd finally make them listen; that she would tell them how she felt. She was going to speak up and be honest and it was

232

going to make her feel good and clean and right.

She didn't anticipate that after everything they've done, she'd somehow still be the one in the wrong.

She's worth enough to tell them her opinion.

"Why are you still here," Lucy pulls herself away from the others, her crying having magically stopped, "if you hate us so much? Haven't you got somewhere better to be – somewhere away from us?"

"I don't *hate* you." Tally speaks slowly, wanting to find the right words and determined to say what she really, truly thinks. "I hate what you *say* sometimes – and what you *do* – but I don't hate you. Sometimes you're not very nice, and I've definitely given you all too many chances to be good friends because I don't think you know what a good friend really looks like, which is sad. But I don't hate you. I just don't like you very much."

Lucy's eyes sparkle, like they're made of metal. "You're going to be sorry you spoke to us like this. I hope it was worth it, Tally, cos you're not going to have *anyone* now and year eight is going to be grim because you're all on your own."

Tally looks at her. "It's been grim with all of you," she tells her. "I'd *rather* be on my own. You might not think I'm worth anything but I'm worth more than this."

And then, with her head held as high as she possibly can, she walks into school and straight to the drama room, where she tells Mrs Jarman that, if it's OK, she really needs to use her Safe Space and that she is probably going to need to stay in there for the foreseeable future.

CHAPTER 25

Cat Appreciation Group Chat

Tally: are you guys there?

Tally: anyone?

Tally: hellooooo? is there anybody out there?

Tally: look, I know I wasn't great before but I'm sorry, ok?

Jade: ...

Gory: ...

Tally: I said I'M SORRY. can you even hear me?

Gory: we can now! jeez – there's no need to shout!

Jade: hey tally! it's good to have you back!

Tally: I've missed you guys

Gory: we've been right here

Tally: I know

Jade: so how's it all going? What have you been

up to?

Tally: a lot. mostly bad.

Gory: tell us. we'll get it.

Tally: I did some stuff I'm not very proud of & then everything went wrong

Jade: do you want to tell us what you did?

Tally: I literally just said that I'm not proud of it. why would I want to tell you? That makes no sense.

Gory: yeah, jade! but also, you have to tell us, tally.

Tally: no I don't. but I can tell you that I'm not friends with lucy and the others any more.

Gory: hallelujah!

Jade: gory! that's not nice. they were tally's friends.

Tally: they weren't, actually. they put a video of me stimming online & everyone at school saw it & made nasty comments.

Gory: …

Jade: I'm so sorry, tally. that's awful.

Gory: …

Tally: thanks. it was pretty terrible but at least I know the truth now. and you know, it's not so bad being on my own.

Gory: …

Jade: is school ok then?

Tally: no. it's actually horrible & I hate it. but being on my own isn't so bad.

Jade: are you still there, gory?

Gory: yeah, I'm here. just don't know what to say about the video thing. it makes me want to punch something really hard.

Tally: thanks, gory. that means a lot. I didn't punch anything but at least I told them how it made me feel. Not that it made any difference – I guess I got the words all wrong, just for a change.

Jade: I hate it when that happens

Gory: me too

Tally: I just wish I could say what I'm feeling in a way that other people can hear, you know? it's the same at home when I'm trying to tell them I can't go to school. it just doesn't come out right. I've got all the words when I'm writing my songs & then they all disappear when I try to talk.

Gory: so maybe you should go around singing at people! they'd have to hear you then!

Jade: *shudders* that's an awful idea, gory! can you imagine having to sing your feelings? I'd never say anything ever again!

Gory: ha! me too. and my voice is so rubbish that

people would put their hands over their ears if I started singing, which wouldn't exactly help with them hearing me, would it?!

Jade: don't worry about it, tally. it's their problem and it's not like we can make people listen to us. we all know that.

Gory: tally?

Jade: tally?

Tally: what if I sing and they actually listen, though? what happens then?

CHAPTER 26

"I'm never going back to school." Tally stares at Mum and Dad, daring them to challenge her. "I don't care what you say or what you do – I'm not setting one foot inside Kingswood Academy ever again."

"But you have to go to school," says Dad, frowning. "It's the law."

Tally shrugs. "Whatever. If you want me to go then you're going to have to literally carry me into the building." She eyeballs him. "And I'll run away as soon as you put me down."

"Nobody is carrying anybody anywhere," says Mum firmly. "And there is definitely no need for any silly talk about running away. Tally, Dad and I need to talk and I think it would be best if you went up to your room for a bit."

Tally nods. "I think that would be best too," she agrees. She has no desire to hear them stressing out, once again, about what they're going to do with her.

She leaves the kitchen and is walking past the living room when she hears a sound. Slowly, she pushes open the door and peers inside, not wanting to go in. She hates having to deal with other people being upset but her sister is crying and Tally can't just walk past.

"What's wrong?" she asks, taking a tentative step inside the room. "Are you feeling unwell?"

Nell looks up. "No," she says in a husky voice, like her throat is sore. Tally hopes that Nell isn't sick – she can't stand the idea of other people's germs floating around, waiting to invade her airspace. "I'm not ill. I'm just sad."

"Oh." Tally stares at her. "Shall I get Mum?"

Nell shakes her head. "No. She can't help with this."

Tally thinks hard. "How about a biscuit?"

Nell's head sinks back into her hands, which is presumably also a *no*. Tally frowns. If getting Mum or a biscuit isn't the solution, then she isn't entirely sure what else she has to offer.

"Why are you sad?" she asks, after a long, drawn-out minute where the only sound is Nell's stifled sobs. "If I know what's making you sad then I can probably solve your problem."

Nell wipes her eyes and takes a deep breath. "If you can solve the problem of my entire life being rubbish then, please, go right ahead." She sits up and looks past Tally, her gaze focused on the wall behind the television. "I had a fight with Rosa and now she's never going to talk to me ever again."

Tally takes a few more steps into the room and perches on the arm of the sofa, still keeping her distance from Nell who, despite her declaration of health, is doing an awful lot of sniffing.

"What was the fight about?" she asks.

"Tyler," says Nell. "I've been hanging out with him even though I knew that Rosa liked him first and now I've ruined our friendship."

"Ugh." Tally rolls her eyes. "Is that it?"

Nell nods. "I thought that Rosa didn't mind but it turns out she's been feeling really upset and I didn't even know."

Tally suppresses a groan. Nell's problem isn't a real problem at all. It's just a boy.

"And now she's never going to talk to me again and I've lost my best friend over someone I don't even think

I like that much." Nell's shoulders slump and she flops back against the cushions. "I've ruined everything and she won't answer my texts or calls and there's nothing I can do."

"Just tell Rosa that you're sorry and that you didn't mean to hurt her and that she's way more important than any *boy*." Tally rubs her hands together, pleased with herself for issuing such excellent advice. "There – all sorted. *Now* do you want a biscuit?"

But Nell is not satisfied. "Didn't you hear me? She won't take my calls and she's leaving me on read whenever I text her."

Tally sighs. "So go and *talk* to her," she says. "Or write her a letter, or something. I don't know!"

Something that Mum says to her all the time pops into her head and she gives Nell a firm look. "Use your words, OK? I know that you know a whole *load* of words cos you're always going on and on about stuff, so just do what you're good at. *Make* Rosa listen to you."

Nell opens her mouth to protest and then closes it again, a thoughtful expression on her face. "That's not a terrible idea," she says, almost to herself. "Maybe I *could* write her a letter. I think she'd like that."

"Of *course* it's not a terrible idea," says Tally indignantly. "It's a brilliant idea, actually."

Nell smiles. "It really is. How are you doing, anyway? I heard Mum and Dad talking about you and school. Have you told them what's going on? Is it honestly that bad?"

Tally stands up. "It's worse," she tells her sister. "And, no, I haven't told them because there's nothing they can do about it. Nobody listens to me when I try to tell them how awful it is and I know that for a fact because if they did then they'd never send me there again."

Nell's face falls. "I'm sorry, Tally," she says quietly. "There's been a lot going on here and at school, and I haven't really been looking out for you, have I?"

Tally shakes her head. "No. You haven't."

"So, tell me what I can do to make up for it." Nell pushes herself out of the chair and faces Tally. "I want to help."

Tally shrugs. "Make them hear me," she says. "*You've* got all the words. Make the kids at school know what it feels like to be singled out for being different. Make Mum and Dad know that if they keep forcing me to go to school then I'm going to shatter into one thousand pieces." She takes a deep breath. "Make everyone understand how it feels to be me."

Nell walks forward and puts her hand gently on Tally's arm. "You can tell them yourself, you know. Like you just told me."

Tally scowls and pulls away. "No, I can't. If I try to explain how I'm feeling the words come out wrong and everyone gets mad at me."

Nell nods. "That does happen quite a lot," she agrees. "Maybe you could practise what you want to say first?"

Tally snorts. "I do that all the time! But unless I'm going to send out a script so that the other person knows what *they're* supposed to say, it doesn't work out."

The room falls silent again, the only sound the ticking of the clock on the wall. Tally watches the specks of dust that are dancing in the light streaming through the window and wishes that it were raining. It always feels wrong to be miserable in the sunshine.

"Maybe you need to find another way to say what you're feeling," says Nell. "You know – like you just told me? Perhaps you could write a letter too?"

"Are you *serious*?" Tally looks at her in horror. "Can you imagine me writing a letter to the rest of year eight, telling them how awful it is to see a video of yourself stimming on the internet? What would I do – read it out to them in the school canteen?"

"Good point," agrees Nell. "Wait – what? What video?"

"It doesn't matter now." Tally dismisses the topic with a flick of her hand. "What I'm *trying* to say is that nobody is going to listen to me if I write a letter."

Nell stares at her for a moment, as if she's thinking something but not saying it. Then she flashes Tally a quick smile.

"I'm going to go and write that letter to Rosa," she tells her. "Then I'm going to take it over to her house."

"Good," says Tally. "That'll definitely work and then you won't cry any more."

Nell heads towards the door, pausing once she gets there. "Tally? Promise me that you'll tell me if you need my help, OK? I'm your big sister – that's what I'm here for."

"I thought you were here just to annoy me," Tally tells her. "But, fine, I promise."

Then Nell has gone and Tally heads out of the living room and into the hall, where she can hear Mum and Dad still talking about the conundrum of her.

"We've got to pursue other options, Jennifer." Dad's voice floats beside her as she walks towards the stairs.

"There's got to be something we can do – we can't let her carry on like this."

"I had the meeting with school today," says Mum and then she can't hear anything else. Not that she needs to hear. They might be trying to understand but while they continue to believe that her being in school is more important than her survival she's never going to be able to find the words to tell them otherwise.

But maybe she can do what Nell said.

Maybe she can find another way to say what she's feeling?

A letter wouldn't work, she knows that. And she could *try* to write a speech, but if anyone interrupted her it would all go wrong. Mum sometimes shows her emotions using paint and a canvas and other people might dance or make things, but Tally wants to use words and there is only one thing she can think of where the words always cooperate and say what she wants them to say; the way Dad has taught her to express herself and the exact thing Gory and Jade suggested as a joke on their group chat.

Upstairs in her room, Tally grabs her notepad and starts to write. The words flow from the end of her pen and by the time she's done, she's found ways of saying things that have only *ever* lived in her head. The tune has been playing in her head for days and it doesn't take long for her to put it all together – lyrics and melody – and then record herself using her phone. She's done this before, lots of times. Written a song, composed the music and then filmed herself playing and singing.

But she's never put it out there before.

She's never shared it with anyone else.

Sending the video to her YouTube account is easy. Finding the courage to make her account public is harder. Her account has always been private but she follows Lucy and some of the other kids in year eight who have YouTube accounts – so now there's a tiny risk that they'll be able to find her too. But if there's even the slightest chance that this will work then she has to try. Tally waits while the video uploads and then, once the song is on her channel, she copies the link and texts it to Mum and Dad.

Then she waits. She's spent the last nearly-thirteen years waiting for someone to properly listen to her and she can wait a little longer. And while she waits, she starts to wonder if maybe this was part of the problem all along. Nobody could hear her because she wasn't sharing what she really felt.

What if it's not about waiting for them all to hear her?

What if instead, it's about not being afraid to use her true voice?

Five tips for aspiring song writers

1. Don't rush! You may suddenly feel like you have to write everything down, but let your experiences and thoughts gently seep out throughout the song for the best results.

2. Don't worry if you get frustrated when you can't think of a rhyme/next lyric/the right chords. Just take a deep breath and know you can always come back to it later.

3. Work on your song when nobody else is around. If you are anything like me, you will feel self-conscious writing a song in front of others. Try having an hour in your own thoughts.

4. Don't let other people's opinions count! No matter what you do or who you are, you are bound to get hate from someone. You could be the most talented person alive and still get negative comments. I mean, look at Taylor Swift!

5. Remember that practice makes perfect. If it's your first time writing a song, it may not quite be "Shake It Off", but, saying that, you never know! The more you work hard at perfecting your talent, the better the results will be.

All The Pieces of Me

My heart is shrivelled, all the joy's squeezed out,
The voices are screaming louder and louder, so loud,
My head keeps turning should I go or should I stay?
The thought of getting myself there, it takes my
breath away

All the pieces of me
Are shattered on the floor
I'm already just fragments of girl
I can't go back for more

I fight with the angels,
While shaking hands with devils
Feels like no one is on my level
Guess I gotta make it clear that

This is not a choice
This is the way that I'm built
So I refuse to let your cold heart fill mine with guilt
Do the most you can is what I like to hear, not
I'm counting to three and then you'd better be here

All the pieces of me
Are shattered on the floor
I'm already just fragments of girl
I can't go back for more

I've lost myself
They made me lose myself
Please don't make me lose myself
No more.

CHAPTER 27

The minutes tick by. Mum and Dad are still in the kitchen and she doesn't know if they've even got their phones with them. Maybe they won't see her message or click the link? Maybe this was a stupid idea?

Tally paces her room, unable to sit still. What was she doing, sharing her song with them? What made her think they'd understand her lyrics when they *clearly* can't understand her when she's right there, telling them how she feels? She shouldn't have done it. It was the wrong decision. Nell didn't know what she was talking about when she suggested Tally find another way to express her emotions – her body talks louder than she does but nobody ever seems to hear her when she's stimming or fighting or frozen or running away. She was foolish to think that *any* words that came out of her mouth could be understood.

She stomps towards the bedroom door, intent on finding Mum and Dad's phones and deleting the link before they can see it. And then her laptop pings with a notification and she glances at the screen.

There is a comment beneath the video of her singing.

Very slowly, she walks closer and peers at the words, holding her breath. If someone has found her account and given her even more hate, then she knows that's it. She'll never write another song again.

But it isn't hate. It's brief and to the point and it's the opposite of hate. It is friendship and understanding, in a few short words, from a most unexpected source.

You're great. Don't let anyone ever make you forget it. See you. Luke ☺

And then there is a gentle knock at her door and Mum and Dad are there, staring at her with a look on their faces that Tally cannot quite fathom.

"It's beautiful, Tally," says Mum. "Heartbreaking, but beautiful."

"Is that how school really makes you feel?" asks Dad.

Tally nods and his face crumples.

"I'm sorry," he says softly. "I knew it was hard but I didn't know how bad."

Tally crosses the room in three long steps and wraps her arms around his waist. "I thought I was telling you," she says. "But I don't think I was. Not really."

Dad hugs her back tightly. "I don't think I was listening," he whispers. "Not really. But I'm listening now, I really am."

Mum wraps her arms around the pair of them and they stand together, holding each other up. Tally knows that everything isn't perfect and that one song isn't going to change the world. She has no idea what's going to happen but at least she has started using her voice in the way that feels right for her, and maybe now she'll be able to share how she's feeling a bit more.

"We need to talk about school," says Mum, when the hug is finally over. "Let's sit down."

She sits on Tally's bed and gestures for Tally to join her. Dad pulls across a chair, and when Mum nods at him, clears his throat and starts to speak.

"We don't want you to feel broken," he says, and Tally can see his eyes filling with tears. "But we also don't want you to miss out on getting an education and doing the things that are going to help you have a great life when you're older."

Tally opens her mouth to tell him that it doesn't matter how much she learns, if she's smashed into pieces of girl then she's never going to have a great life – but then she closes it again. He heard her song. He knows.

"So, we've been looking into some ways that you can keep learning but not have to deal with school," says Mum, picking up the conversation. "So far, you've been going to the stables for a bit of time out, but Ginny offers quite a lot more than that." She pauses and looks carefully at Tally. "Some kids get to go there for a few days every week and look after the horses and learn to ride while doing other things too."

"What other things?" asks Tally. "What else can you do at the stables?"

Dad leans forward. "Ginny runs an alternative education programme. Mum's been finding out about it. Kids who attend get to do all the usual stable activities but there's a qualified teacher on-site who does other things."

"Like lessons?" Tally is suspicious. School is still school, no matter where it is.

"A bit," agrees Mum. "For example, they do maths but it's mostly connected to the horses – so you might weigh them and plot the results on a graph or work out the amount of food they need using ratios – that kind of stuff. It's really hands-on and practical and everything they learn is for a reason."

"Why haven't you sent me there already?" asks Tally. "It sounds good."

Dad looks at Mum, his eyes clouded. "We didn't want to give up on the idea of you being in school," he says. "We thought it would get better."

"It's getting worse," Tally informs him. "So, can I go there?"

Mum puts her arm around Tally. "We need the school on board first and then we need to talk to the local authority to see if they'll pay for your place, but we're working on that. If they both agree, you'll go to the stables on some days and on other days you'll have a tutor come here to work with you at home. You'd be with other kids at the stables so you wouldn't get lonely and then you'd have some space to work on more typical schoolwork here, without all the pressures of being in school."

"It wouldn't have to be for ever," adds Dad. "Lots of

kids do this kind of thing for a year or so and then feel a bit more confident about going back into school."

Tally pauses, thinking about it.

No sitting in the classroom with the harsh lights that hurt her eyes and make her head pound.

No navigating the corridors, trying to remember where she's supposed to be next.

No more spending every second of the school day focused on what people want her to say or do.

No waking up feeling sick with fear before she's even opened her eyes.

"Have a think about it," says Mum. "There's no need to make a decision now, and we still have to convince the school."

"I'll convince them," murmurs Dad. "I'll show them the song if that's what it takes. We can't let you carry on feeling like this. I can see that now."

But Tally doesn't need to think about it. There are some good things about school, she knows that. The library and her Safe Space and Mrs Jarman. And not *all* of the kids are awful. She's been sitting next to Millie in science lessons and that's been good. But it won't be for ever, like Dad said – and school isn't going anywhere. It would be so, so good to have some time to figure out who she is and what she wants without constantly having to worry about who everyone else wants her to be. Maybe she can take a break from school and then, when she's ready to go back, it won't be so difficult to handle.

Maybe she'll be heard.

CHAPTER 28

The relief is immense. Even though nothing is certain, as Mum keeps on reminding her, Tally knows deep down that it's all going to work out. It *has* to – she's finally found a way to use her voice, and that has made everything start to change. Which is why it's strange that she still can't sleep, despite telling herself over and over again that all her problems are sorted.

She tries *everything*. Counting the ridiculous jumping sheep and trying the mindful meditation app that Mum put on her phone a few weeks ago, but nothing works. Tally lies in the darkness and stares at her jellyfish lamp, watching them float aimlessly without any intent or purpose. And then it hits her. The reason she can't sleep is because she feels bad and this particular flavour of *bad* has got nothing to do with horrible videos or Lucy and the others or the stress of homework deadlines or conversations that make no sense.

This particular bad feeling has got guilt running right through its middle.

Tally gets up and turns on her desk lamp. There are two people living in her head and she knows that she won't be able to get any peace until she makes it better with them.

Until she does the right thing.

The first song is for Annie and it feels easy to write. The words pour out as she scribbles down her thoughts about the Unicorn Rainbow Girl who seems able to put her own values above her need to belong. And as she writes, Tally starts to see something new. Annie isn't an outsider and she isn't alone. She's just not prepared to follow the herd. She's an explorer, forging ahead and figuring things out for herself.

Maybe being alone is not the same thing as being lonely?

Perhaps every group needs people who don't always want to flock together; people who will venture out and look at the world a little differently?

What if the herd can only survive because of the

people who will dare to go to the edges and stray a bit further?

People like Annie.

People like Millie.

People like Tally?

Tally writes and she sings and she pours out her heart and then, once she's recorded her song and put it on her channel, she finds Annie's profile on Instagram and sends her the link. She doesn't know what the other girl will think and she has no clue if she'll even bother to listen to what Tally is saying, but it feels good to have put herself out there.

And then it's time to write the second song and this one is far more of a challenge. She's told Millie several times how sorry she is for what she did, but saying it is only one part of making things right and sorry is only one word; she needs to let Millie know that she *understands* how badly she hurt her. The words stutter and stumble from the end of her pen and she scratches most of them out, trying to find the right phrases to explain. She doesn't want to make excuses or turn the hurt back on to her – she caused Millie pain and she needs to admit that, but it's hard.

So, so hard.

Eventually it's done. The melody is low, with a slow, steady tempo which weaves and dips around Tally's voice. She uploads the video and then copies the link before opening her messenger app. They've sent each other a couple of messages about the science homework before and so Tally finds their chat and pastes in the link, pausing for a second to debate whether she should include a greeting or an explanation. But she's all out of words and if the song isn't enough to show Millie that she's sorry then she isn't sure what else she can do. She sends the message and then closes her laptop. It's three o'clock in the morning and she's drained and exhausted but her head is finally quiet.

She can let herself go to sleep.

Tally sleeps in late the next morning and it isn't until Nell slams the front door on her way out that she wakes. She stretches, prodding the corners of her brain to see if the feeling is there, before remembering that it's OK. Nobody is going to force her to go into school. She doesn't have to fight to survive, not today.

Smiling, she throws back her duvet and swings her legs off the mattress. Billy, her favourite cuddly toy, has fallen on to the floor in the night and she rescues him before heading across to her laptop and opening the screen. The notifications button tells her that she has one new comment and she clutches Billy tightly with one hand as the other clicks on the video she sent to Annie. The other girl doesn't have to be nice, Tally knows that. It's not as if Tally has exactly gone out of her way to be kind to her and it's probably too much to ask that they could ever be friends.

But the comment below the video is more than she could have possibly hoped for. Tally reads it through a first time and then a second, a smile growing across her face and spreading down into her chest, her stomach, her toes.

This is brilliant, Tally! I love it! Please can I share it on my page? Looking forward to hanging out on the edges with you soon – message me, OK?

She *gets* it. Annie heard her song and she understands what Tally was trying to tell her. Hanging out on the edges and exploring loudly with Annie sounds like a whole lot more fun than being embroiled in the centre of Lucy's group, passive and silent and still.

There's no message from Millie and even though Tally knows she has no right to expect a response, she's still disappointed. Pocketing her phone, she goes downstairs and into the kitchen where Mum is making a cup of tea.

"Morning!" she says. "Did you sleep well?"

Tally nods. There's no need to tell Mum that she was up half the night, and, anyway, it isn't a lie because once she *did* get to sleep, her dreams were calm.

"I thought you could go over to the stables this morning," Mum tells her. "And this afternoon we need to pop into school to pick up some more schoolwork for you to do."

Tally nods again. She'd rather spend the whole day at the stables but Mum is still working on sorting out the funding and she's made it very clear that if Tally doesn't do the work she's being set by her teachers, there's no way that they'll agree to her being educated out of school.

"Excellent!" Mum smiles. "In that case, you grab something to eat and I'll just get a few jobs done before I run you up to Ginny's." She picks up her tea and walks out of the kitchen, leaving Tally to contemplate the most important decision of the day and choose what to have for breakfast.

She's just finished spreading honey on her toast when her phone pings. She takes a bite and then pulls it from her pocket. It's a message and the contents make her smile so widely that her cheeks ache.

This is great! You can officially stop apologizing to me now, OK? Millie

Her time at the stables with Nigel flies by and Mum is back before she's ready to leave. The drive to school is faster than she'd like and it feels only seconds before Mum is pulling into the car park and ushering her from the car.

"Why can't I just stay here?" moans Tally, dragging her feet as they approach the main entrance. "You can collect the work for me."

"Well, firstly, I'm not your servant," Mum points out. "And, secondly, some of your teachers want to see you. I know that your maths teacher wants to explain what you need to do."

"She's rubbish at explaining," Tally mutters. "Why can't *you* just help me?"

"*I* am not a maths teacher," Mum mumbles, smiling at the receptionist behind the desk. "And remember what I said about showing them you can work well in a different environment? Part of that includes listening to what the teachers are saying when they give you the work."

Tally pulls a face, but Mum is too busy talking in the voice she uses when she really wants to impress someone to notice. Tally wanders across the hall to look at the display cabinet and then the bell rings and before she can make it back to Mum, hordes of kids are streaming out of doors and through the hall, their voices loud and clamouring above the piercing, relentless bell.

"You're back, then?"

They're suddenly there, right in her face. Lucy, Ayesha and Jasmine, arms linked and eyes narrowed.

"No." Tally is quiet and there's no way they can hear her over the noise, but they read her lips and frown.

"What's wrong with you?" demands Ayesha. "How come your mum is talking to Mr Kennedy?"

"You'd better not have snitched on us," snarls Lucy. "It's not our problem if you can't take a joke. *Weirdo*."

Tally closes her eyes and counts to three, but when she opens them again the girls are still there, their hot breath wafting towards her and making her not want to breathe.

"You're right," she says, and this time her voice is loud, loud enough to make the people walking past stop and listen. "It's not *your* problem. It's *my* problem. You are *all* my problem and I'm finally doing something about it."

"You tell them!" someone calls and when Tally turns to look, she sees Luke nodding at her. "Someone's got to. They're getting properly harsh and none of us like it."

"She owned you there, Lucy!" yells Ameet. "You're one great big problem!"

A ripple of laughter flows through the throng of people pushing past and Tally tenses.

"Don't call Tally *weird*." Millie steps out of the crowd and glares at Lucy. "It's rude and offensive and, honestly, it makes you look completely ignorant."

Lucy's face flushes deep red.

"I warned you once before," she hisses at Tally. "Someone like *you* doesn't get to talk to people like *us* in this way."

"Yeah, well, she just did so get over yourself." Ayesha and Jasmine are shoved aside as a mass of rainbow-coloured hair pushes past them. "And, for the record,

I think most people here would rather be someone like Tally than be part of anything that you stand for."

Annie grabs Tally's hand and starts to pull her away from the display cabinet. "Come on, your mum is looking for you."

Tally flashes a grateful smile at Millie and then turns, forcing Annie to stop walking. Furious muttered threats are spewing from Lucy's mouth but she's safe now.

"You know, you really should work on your insults," she tells Lucy. "The number of times you have called me *weird* over the past two years suggests that you have a very limited repertoire."

Annie tugs her arm and together they start to move across the entrance hall. They can't do anything else to hurt her. She doesn't have to deal with them ever again.

"Use your words!" she yells, over the heads of the passing kids. "Use. Your. Damn. Words!"

News Report: Tally Turns into a Tiger

Well, that felt good. Strange, and exhausting, but good. When I first started this school, I used to wear a tiger mask a lot of the time at home. But I never wore it at school. I wore a different mask, the one of the "perfect kid" trying to fit in. Today, I peeled off that mask, and it turns out there's another tiger underneath – a real one this time. I wonder if it's been there all along, just waiting to emerge and be heard and seen.

Imagine if everyone at school – teachers and kids – spent a week as an autistic person. They would soon stop seeing us as "different" and would start to realize how much we have to endure each day – from the noise and busyness, to the pressure to conform and the endless rules ... it's so much to deal with.

If autistic people designed schools, just imagine how amazing they would be...

What is the dream classroom for an autistic kid? (Well, this autistic kid anyway.)

It's all about the senses, and how I feel when I walk in there.

What does it look like?

- Lighting: warm white fairy lights hanging all around – no awful, noisy, blinding strip lights, but instead maybe interesting lamps, like lava lamps or colour-changing lamps.
- Walls: painted in calming colours, like pale blue, neutral colours, light greens, greys, pale pinks. Decorated with pictures, inspirational quotes, lyrics from Taylor Swift songs.
- Lots of big plants with interesting leaves.
- Vases of flowers that smell nice, like hyacinths.
- A huge TV playing scenes from nature, like amazing views.
- Lots of things that feel natural.

What does it sound like?

- The soft furnishings, like rugs, cushions, etc, soak up sound.

- There's music playing quietly in the background. Relaxing jazz piano, or sounds of nature, like rain. Maybe even both together.
- A water feature, like a little fountain or waterfall, makes soothing trickling sounds.

What does it smell like?
- Aromatherapy oils that aren't overpowering.
- Baking bread. Kneading dough each day would be good for stress relief too.
- Fresh herbs like basil and coriander.
- Greenery – the earthy smell of real plants. Ooh, and real grass!

What does it feel like?
- Stimmy things like sequinned pillows where you can change the colour by brushing them a different way.
- Comfy, with lots of things to sit on, like cushions and beanbags.
- Snug, with blankets and cushions in fabrics that feel nice, like fur, satin and velvet.
- You can walk around in socks or bare feet.

What is there to do when you are stressed?

- A hanging stretchy hammock to get into when you feel over-stimulated.
- A tent to lie down in when you need to get away from it all.
- A weighted blanket for calming down with.
- An egg chair with a lid you can pull down over you.
- A selection of fidget toys to choose from.
- An awesome slime collection – cloud slime, fluffy slime, butter slime, crunchy slime, clear slime, jiggly slime, fishbowl slime, cupcake slime...

CHAPTER 29

"I'm not eating that." Tally folds her arms across her chest and glares at Mum. "It's disgusting and slimy and you can't make me."

"It's lasagne," says Mum, sounding confused. "You normally like lasagne."

But just because Tally usually eats lasagne, doesn't mean that she's going to be able to eat it every single time Mum cooks it, for the rest of her life.

Things change.

People change.

"You and Dad normally like each other," Tally points out, trying to make her understand. "But sometimes you argue and get cross about stuff and then you don't like each other at all."

"That's not true," splutters Dad. "And it's completely

irrelevant to this conversation."

"How?" Tally turns her laser stare on to him. "How is it irrelevant? Sometimes you and Mum like each other and sometimes you don't. Well – that's how I feel about lasagne."

She leans back in her chair, confident that this time she's found the right way to explain her cause. The rest of the table sit in silence, their mouths slightly gaping and their eyes staring at her with something that looks maybe like shock, but that can't be right because she hasn't said anything they didn't already know.

"Girls, I hope you know that even if Dad and I are cross that we still love each other very much," says Mum eventually.

Nell makes a groaning sound and puts down her fork. "Do we have to do this now?"

"I just want you to understand that however tough things might feel at times, we're a great team and there's a lot of love in this house," reiterates Mum.

"Absolutely," says Dad.

"Okaaaaay," says Tally slowly. "I actually said that sometimes you don't *like* each other. I didn't even think that you wouldn't ever *love* each other but now you're going on about it, I'm kind of wondering why you'd even bring it up."

Nell mutters a rude word under her breath but nobody except Tally hears her.

"Shall we just eat our supper?" suggests Dad. "What were we talking about before the conversation got derailed?"

"Lasagne," Tally reminds him. "How I don't like lasagne like Mum sometimes doesn't like you, and when you leave the house she sometimes pulls a horrid face at the front door when you can't see her."

"Toast!" Mum leaps up, her chair scraping against the kitchen floor. "How about we forget all about the lasagne and you have a lovely piece of toast instead?"

Tally thinks about it. "I like toast. Yes, please." She turns to Dad. "Do you *always* like Mum, then?"

Nell's head flops into her hands. "Can I eat in my room?" she begs. "Please?"

"Yes, I always like your mother," Dad replies, shooting a smile at Mum as she rams a piece of bread into the toaster.

"Thanks," she calls back. "I quite like you too."

"*Always?*" persists Tally. "So you never, ever think she's a bit of pain? Because that's OK, you know. You don't have to like something all the time. You're allowed to change your mind."

Dad looks a bit flustered. "I mean – I guess we fall out now and then and I don't like *that*. And when you become parents you end up having all these huge things that you have to make decisions about and it's really hard because all you want to do is get it right but you don't know what *right* looks like so sometimes you get cross with each other and say a whole load of stuff when really you should be listening to what the other person is trying to tell you."

Mum walks over to the table and places a hand on Dad's shoulder, giving it a gentle squeeze. "That's true," she agrees. "But we always, always have love, even if we're struggling to hear each other. Don't you think, Kevin?"

"Absolutely," he says, reaching up to put his hand on top of Mum's. "And the wonderful thing about love is that it doesn't matter if someone is annoying you or you don't necessarily agree with them. Because love has many layers – and those layers grow as your relationship grows and you come to realize that, really it doesn't matter if—"

"Don't overcomplicate it, Kevin," mutters Mum out of the corner of her mouth.

"You're right." Dad puts some food in his mouth. "Jennifer – this lasagne is exceptional. As are you."

Tally considers telling him not to talk with his mouth full because it's disgusting, but the way his eyes are sparkling when he looks at Mum makes her pause.

Mum laughs and heads back towards the toaster. "Why, thank you. You're not too terrible yourself."

Tally rolls her eyes and waits patiently for her toast to arrive. Life is already confusing enough – why adults seem so determined to make it even trickier is a mystery to her and one that she doesn't think she will ever solve.

Upstairs in her room, Tally scrolls through her phone. She's finally got a message from Layla telling her about her new school in Florida and how much she misses Tally and that it's taken forever for her parents to sort her out with a phone which is why she hasn't messaged before. There's another message too from Annie, asking her if she wants to hang out with her and Millie on Saturday morning at the zoo. Tally loves that place but there's no way she could have admitted that to the girls – only little kids and old people ever visit the zoo and suggesting a trip there would have resulted in a lot of ridicule.

Her phone beeps with a notification and Tally sees

that she's been tagged in a post on Instagram. She grins and swipes the screen, expecting to see a cute picture of a kitten (Jade's usual posts) or a frantic dance video (Gory's preferred content). But it isn't either of those things. It's the last thing she expects to see and at the same time it feels completely, one hundred per cent, inevitable.

It's another video.

And once again, she has the starring role.

It's already playing and Tally watches as the girl on the screen flaps her arms and blinks her eyes and shifts nervously from one foot to the other. The footage has been sped up and her limbs are a whirl of movement as she points at someone off-screen, her mouth moving in overdrive. Her phone is on mute and she clicks the icon, letting her sped-up, high-pitched voice fill the room.

You are all my problem you are all my problem you are all my problem.

Someone filmed her when she went into school. It can't have been Lucy or the others because she'd have seen them, but whoever it was has clearly given it to them, because the accompanying caption has definitely been written by Lucy, despite the fact that this has been posted to an anonymous account.

Just so you're all aware: Tally Adams
thinks that we are all her problem! She
hates everyone, which is nice, when all any
of us have tried to do is to be kind to her
even though she doesn't really fit in.

As Tally watches, the comments start. And this time they're worse than before. It's as if whatever Lucy says is instantly heard and everyone just believes her – even when they know that it can't be true. Tally puts down her phone and tries to stay calm.

This doesn't matter to her.

This *shouldn't* matter to her.

The people who care about her know that this isn't what she meant. Let them think the worst of her; let them believe Lucy when she tells them that Tally is different, a misfit. Who cares?

Tally cares. She cares a lot but not about what she cared about before. She doesn't want to be part of anything that costs more than she's willing to pay and she's trying not to mind if someone doesn't like her, even though it still hurts. What she cares about most is not letting another person get away with speaking on her behalf. This time she cannot stay silent while they all judge her. This time she has got to speak up.

Quickly, before she can change her mind, she picks up her phone and sends a message to her friends – her real friends. She texts Gory and Jade and Layla. She messages Annie and Millie and, after a moment of hesitation, sends a text to Luke too. It can't hurt. And then she sits down at her desk and stares at herself in the mirror. Her hair is a state and her cheeks are flushed with nerves and there's a very real chance that she might start crying if she gives herself any time to think, but that's just the way it's going to have to be.

"Hey." Nell pushes open her door and leans on the frame. "What are you doing?"

Tally opens her mouth to tell her to get lost and then pauses. Nell said she'd help if she ever needed it and Tally needs help now, more than ever.

"There's a video of me online," she tells her. "It makes me look kind of bad."

Nell pulls out her own phone and scrolls quickly through the screens. Tally looks away, trying to keep her breathing under control while she sets up her keyboard. She knows when Nell has found the video, partly because of the distorted sound of her voice filling the room and partly because of the slew of curses that pour from Nell's lips. She strides across the room and stares at Tally in the mirror.

"This is not OK," she says, her voice low. "But don't worry – I'm going to handle it."

And it would be so, so good to crawl into bed and let her big sister deal with the bullies and the unkind and the cruel. But she can't do that.

"I'm handling it myself." Tally's eyes link with Nell's reflection. "You *can* help me, though. I've sent a message to my friends, asking them to tell people to check out my Insta account, but the problem is that they don't actually have many friends to share it with." She spins round and looks at Nell. "*You* know loads of people. Will you tell them what I'm doing and get them to watch?"

Nell frowns, her eyebrows pulling tightly together. "What exactly *are* you doing?" she asks.

Tally turns back to her phone and pulls up her account. "I'm going to perform a live song," she says, her stomach flipping over as the words leave her mouth. "I can't *tell* everyone that Lucy is wrong about me but I can *show* them. They have to find me first, though – nobody will hear me if they don't even know that I'm making a noise."

Nell stares at her and Tally crosses her fingers. And then she nods. "Fine – I'll share your account with everyone I know, and then after this I'm going to make sure you're on a private setting, OK?"

Tally uncrosses her fingers and smiles up at Nell. "Thank you. Now go away because I need to start."

Nell snorts and then bends down, pulling Tally into a hug.

"If this doesn't work then I'm dealing with it my way," she murmurs. "Just so you know."

"Your way sounds like it could be dangerous," says Tally, pulling out of Nell's grasp.

"Only for them." Nell gives her a nod and then she's gone, the door closed behind her and the room silent. Tally takes a deep breath, positions her phone behind her keyboard and then she clicks on the Live recording button.

"I'm Tally," she says hesitantly. "And I'm not that great at explaining how I feel so I'm going to sing a song about it instead."

And then she plays the opening chords and starts to sing the song that she wrote in the darkest days after Lucy shared the first video. Everything else fades into the distance; the phone and the camera and making herself more vulnerable than she's ever been – none of it matters. She gets lost in the words and her voice soars with the music and for the first time, Tally Olivia Adams shares how she's really feeling with anyone who will listen.

And it feels wonderful.

CHAPTER 30

It's done. Tally sings the final note and then glances at the counter, which shows the number of people who have joined her live feed. It's not thousands. It isn't even hundreds. But it isn't zero. She stares at the screen, wondering what she's supposed to do now. There are people out there and they're listening.

Nell dashes into the room and reaches over her shoulder to stop the recording.

"That was *amazing*," she breathes, her fingers moving fast as she does something with the phone.

Tally nods. "There were fifteen people watching me," she informs Nell, her voice proud.

Nell laughs. "There're going to be a lot more than that in a minute," she says. "There!" She clicks on the screen and Tally's page refreshes, this time with her video at the top. "I've posted the replay video into your profile. Now everyone who looks at your account can watch it again. Look – someone's leaving a comment."

Both girls lean forward and look at the flickering dots on the screen, holding their breath. And then the words appear, followed by another comment and then another and Nell sighs in relief.

Tally, on the other hand, is too stunned to breathe.

God – I totally get what you're saying.

You have a great voice – why don't you sing like this at school?

I feel like this too. Thanks for being brave enough to share.

I didn't think anyone else felt this way.

Excellent video – well done!

She turns to Nell, her eyes shining.

"Is this really happening?" she whispers. "How are so many people finding me?"

Nell grins down at her. "I had a few friends share it on their socials."

Tally shakes her head in amazement and looks back at her phone as a new comment pops up.

We can hear you, Tally

It's from Luke. The same Luke who once caused her to have the biggest meltdown she's ever had at school, and her most unlikely ally, and the genuine evidence that sometimes, just sometimes, people can be better.

She stares at the screen as the number of views on her video continues to climb and the comments keep on coming.

"Thank you," she tells Nell. "You made this happen."

"No, I didn't." Nell gives her a nod and then heads back towards the door. "I told some people about it and got them to check out your video. But *you're* the reason they stayed to listen. You did that all by yourself, Tally."

She opens the door and then turns. "You've got two hours to enjoy this," she warns. "And then I'm coming back to make your account private. You can still put videos on there but you need to choose who you want to see them, OK? It needs to be just for your actual friends, not any randoms who stumble across you."

Tally nods. She's just had a thought and, as Nell leaves the room, she navigates to the anonymous profile that posted the video of her. Scrolling down, she sees there have been several new comments since she last looked and all of them are telling whoever is hiding behind the fake profile picture to stop being such a coward and either reveal their identity or remove the video. That's not what she's here to see, though. What she wants is a number. She wants to know how many people have watched the video of her in the school corridor and when her eyes land on the figure, her heart skips a beat.

She's done it. More people wanted to listen to her song than to watch an unkind, untrue clip of her on a loop. Whatever happens now, she has been louder than the haters. She'll let Nell make her account private because, while the knowledge that she's worked out a way to be heard is truly wonderful, she doesn't need the whole world to keep listening.

It's enough that, now, she can hear herself.

EPILOGUE

Tally cannot remember a time when she wasn't shovelling dirty, stinking hay into a wheelbarrow. It's a scorching hot day and the sweat is running down her face but she can't stop. She *won't* stop until Nigel has a fresh, clean stall to sleep in tonight. It's the least she can do after he let her ride him all the way to the top field and back again earlier this afternoon.

The sound of singing floats through the stables, getting louder as Ginny approaches. Tally grins to herself. Ginny has a terrible singing voice, although Tally would never tell her that. The worst thing you can possibly do to a person is stop them from expressing themselves, whatever that might sound or look like.

"How are you getting on in there?" Ginny pauses by the gate and peers in at Tally. "You've got a maths lesson in a few minutes so you might want to stop and have a drink before you have to get your brain in gear."

Tally shovels the last of the dirty hay into the barrow and then straightens up, her back aching. She didn't ever think that there would come a time when she was excited about doing maths, but the teacher at the stables has set up a jumping course in the paddock and today they're going to walk around, calculating how many strides each horse will need to take between every jump. And tomorrow, Ginny is going to take them out, one at a time, to have their first experience of riding through the course – so the maths really matters because if she gets it wrong then Nigel will knock the post off every jump.

Outside, the sun is beating down but there's a bit of shade at the front of the building. Tally takes her water bottle and sits down, watching as Ginny helps Jasper, one of the other kids, clamber on to Shadow. Jasper hasn't ever spoken to anyone at the stables and he's usually in a pretty foul mood when he arrives, but Tally has seen the way he calms down once he's with the horse and she's definitely heard him talking to Shadow when they've both been mucking out in the stables. She's not sure that any of the adults even know that Jasper can speak but she hasn't told anyone.

It's *his* voice. He gets to decide when to use it.

Later, as the sun is starting to set, Mum arrives to collect Tally. She gets out of the car and leans on the paddock fence, watching as Tally finishes her final calculations in preparation for tomorrow's jumping course. Tally hands her clipboard to the teacher and then heads over to Mum. Things have been much calmer at home since she stopped going to school, and there's less yelling and more laughing, which is definitely a good thing. Mum and Dad have tried to talk to Tally about what might happen in the future but she puts her hands over her ears and blocks them out. Sometimes adults want to tell you stuff that you just don't need to hear and Tally isn't daft. She knows that nothing lasts for ever, but she's trying to do what people are always telling her to do by not worrying about it for now.

Her phone beeps as Mum pulls out of the farm gates and on to the main road. Tally looks down at the message and grins. Ever since she set it up, the Rainbow Unicorn Appreciation Chat has been a complete success and tonight is the inaugural meeting of the group at her house. Annie and Millie haven't met Gory and Jade in person yet, but Tally knows it's going to be great, because they all believe the same thing:

Sometimes, you have to speak out. No matter who might be listening or how hard it might be. Because you have things to say and ideas to share and speeches to make and if you can't even listen to yourself, then you can't expect anyone else to listen either.

You need to tell your stories in whatever way works best for you. You can use words or music or art or movement. You can sing or sign or use a device or symbols. It doesn't really matter as long as you keep on sharing the wonderful, unique thoughts that are in your head.

Because everyone deserves to be heard.

Tally deserves to be heard.

You deserve to be heard.

And we can hear you.

Can You Hear Me?

They tried to kick me to the floor
And I went back again for more
They hurt so much
I just couldn't ignore
But it's OK now cos I'm as loud as I can be
I'm a tiger, tiger, tiger set free
But we can be tigers, tigers, tigers, you and me
I'm a survivor

Can you see me? I'm right here.
Can you hear me when I'm there?
I'm trying to make myself as loud as I can be
Will you be here when I'm down?
Will you cheer me, when
I frown?
Or will you *smile* when I frown?
Will you still be here when I'm as loud as I can be?

I've moved on from the past
Can I make these good times last?
They mean so much
I wanna keep them coming fast

292

But if not, I'm still as loud as I can be
I'm a survivor, that's me
We are survivors, you and me

Can you see me? I'm right here.
Can you hear me when I'm there?
I'm trying to make myself as loud as I can be.
Will you be here when I'm down?
Will you cheer me, when
I frown?
Will you still be here when I'm as loud as I can be?

AUTISM SPECIAL:
Things well-meaning people say or do that can hurt an autistic person

Hesitate or lower your voice when saying the word "autism" or "autistic"

I know you are trying to be kind or discreet, but it's like you are talking about some kind of disease. And it's almost as bad as saying that I "suffer" with autism, or using "on the spectrum" as a euphemism. C'mon, let's just say the word, people. AUTISTIC. There – it's not so bad, is it? This is especially crucial if you're still learning to love the word "autistic". And do you know why that's so important? Because if you're autistic like me, then loving autism means loving yourself. And that means loving the person you actually are, not the person others think you should be.

"Are we using our autism as a bit of an excuse?"

This was an actual phrase said to me by someone. It's bad on two levels. First of all, autism is a reason not an excuse. Secondly, why do people say we when they mean you? My mum says it's a bit patronizing.

"You can't say autistic. People with autism are people first."

Surely I can use any term I like to describe myself? I already know I'm a person. I just don't like it sounding as if autism is something I carry around with me or is a horrible disease.

"You've got to stop worrying so much about everything."

That's not very helpful. And it makes me worry about worrying, which means that the worries will never stop.

"All twelve-year-old girls get anxious."

Maybe, but autism is something different, so if you say this to me it makes me feel like you are not listening, or like you are making light of how hard life is for me. Also when you make out that everyone feels like me, but they are just getting on with it, it is basically saying it's my fault, and that I must just be dealing with it badly.

"No one likes doing things other people ask them to do."

Same as above.

"No one likes change"

Same as above.

"We're all a bit autistic."

Oh this old gem. No we aren't. Autistic traits are human traits, but it's the grouping and intensity of them that makes a person autistic. When people say things like, "We're all a bit autistic", they're trying to empathize and say that a lot of people struggle with things, but this makes light of what autistic people feel and go through, and I think it's important that people try not to do that.

Acknowledgements

Libby would like to thank her mum, dad and sister Rosie, as well all the rest of her family for the support they continue to give her.

Special thanks to Julia from CAMHS who helped me through the difficult last 2 years, and to The Link at Bromley's Hospital Tutoring Service, which gave me a light at the end of the tunnel when school proved too much.

And thank you to Ava and Lola for being there.

Libby and Rebecca would like to share their gratitude for the wonderful support and patience from Fiz Osborne at Scholastic and Julia Churchill at A M Heath. It's incredible to be part of such an amazing team.